"DROP THE RIFLE
OR YOU'RE BUZZARD BAIT!"

Slocum looked over his shoulder and saw Buck Johnson in the doorway to the cantina. The Arizona Ranger had six-shooters in each hand.

"Good-bye," the Ranger said, both pistols coming up.

"No need," said Slocum. He dropped his rifle and turned. As he did so, he elbowed his skittish horse. The paint reared. In that instant, Slocum went for his Colt Navy.

Slocum saw a red blossom grow on the Arizona Ranger's right side. Then everything was obscured by twin clouds of gunsmoke from Johnson's pistols.

Fiery lead tore through John Slocum's upper body. He doubled over in pain, and the hot desert sand became even hotter when his face pressed into it.

OTHER BOOKS BY JAKE LOGAN

JAKE LOGAN

MEXICAN SILVER

BERKLEY BOOKS, NEW YORK

MEXICAN SILVER

A Berkley Book / published by arrangement with
the author

PRINTING HISTORY
Berkley edition / November 1989

ISBN: 0-425-11838-X

A BERKLEY BOOK ® TM 757,375
Berkley Books are published by The Berkley Publishing Group,
200 Madison Avenue, New York, New York 10016.
The name "BERKLEY" and the "B" logo
are trademarks belonging to Berkley Publishing Corporation.

PRINTED IN THE UNITED STATES OF AMERICA

10 9 8 7 6 5 4 3 2 1

1

"It'll be easy as lickin' butter off a knife," Ogelvie declared. "You know it will be!" The tall, scrawny man scratched idly at the pink scar on his left cheek. John Slocum had wondered how he had come by the wound, but he knew better than to ask. For all Ogelvie's easy ways, the man was a cold-blooded killer.

"They got guards in the damn bank," complained Delling. The smaller, plumper man never saw the good points to any plan. He fidgeted and looked for all the world as if he wanted to bolt and run like a scalded dog. He wouldn't have gotten more than a couple of paces. The fourth man sitting around the guttering campfire, Josh Ballard, played with his lariat. He had ridden up from Texas a few months back, he'd claimed, fresh off working the XIT. He idly swung the loop of rope over his head, the sharp swishing noise spooking Delling even more.

From Ballard's looks, Slocum figured he had worked the XIT, all right, but as a rustler.

"It looks good to me," Slocum said. After that no one

said anything. The brisk, cold wind off the Arizona desert blew away all objections after he'd spoken. It was almost ten minutes later when Delling screwed up his courage enough to speak.

"How are we gonna do it? I mean, they got armed *guards* in the damned bank!"

"You worry about the guards too much," said Ogelvie. He scratched himself some more and lay back across his saddle. "Let me and Slocum take care of them. You and Ballard will go through the tellers' cages and scoop up the money."

"Won't be nothing there but greenbacks. Filthy luck," grumbled Ballard.

"He's right. We won't get any gold or silver. They've only got scrip in that bank to pay off the miners."

"You want in or not, Delling?" Ogelvie spoke softly, but the menace in his voice let the others know what Delling's fate was likely to be if he decided to deal himself out.

Ogelvie would deal him out of the game—permanently. Nobody but the hungry coyotes would ever find Delling's grave here on the barren desert.

"We need four men to do the job right," Slocum said. His voice matched Ogelvie's in menace. The two had butted heads more than once, and Slocum had always prevailed. This time he wasn't so sure he wanted to argue much with the tall, thin man. Delling was getting to be a pain in the ass with his constant bitching.

"We—never mind," Ogelvie said suddenly. He saw the coldness in Slocum's green eyes and backed down again. Slocum silently vowed never to turn his back on Ogelvie. The man carried a heavy reputation of having taken out twelve men. Slocum suspected, if the stories were even half true, that Ogelvie had shot most of them in the back. After the Nogales bank robbery, he intended to part company and ride on out to the ocean. He hadn't been to California in a while and had been fighting the bit to see new territory.

Mostly, Slocum wanted to be rich and away from these three. He had joined up with them a week earlier outside Tucson after meeting them in an all-night poker game in the Blue Balls Saloon. He hadn't any intention of robbing a bank then, but the idea had gradually come to them as a group and had increasingly seemed a good one. Slocum had done a fair share of thievin' in his day and wasn't adverse to doing a bit more right now. The jobs had been few and far between in Arizona Territory, and the lawmen had been worse than flies around a rotting corpse.

Ogelvie stood and stretched. Slocum couldn't help thinking that if the man would shut one eye he'd look like a needle. The speed with which Ogelvie whipped out his six-shooter took Slocum by surprise. His own hand only got halfway to his cross-draw holster where his Colt Navy rested easily.

"Don't shoot me!" screeched Delling.

"I didn't mean to spook you none," said Ogelvie. The leer on his lips told a different story. "I was just showing you how simple it's gonna be. We ride into a sleepy little town, and we ride out a heap richer. What could be simpler than that?"

"Nothing," Delling said in a choked voice. He looked to Ballard and Slocum for help. Ballard pointedly glanced away, intent on coiling his rope. Slocum pushed himself to a full sitting position, his eyes never leaving Ogelvie's. His hand rested easily on the butt of his own six-shooter. If Slocum had seen even a hint of murder there, he'd have finished going for his own pistol. The wildness didn't speak of death—but it didn't speak too loudly about sanity, either.

"No need to get yourself riled, Slocum," Ogelvie said. He sank back to the ground and warmed his hands in front of the small cooking fire. "We got to do this together, just as you said. It'll take four of us. We got everything straight?"

"We know what's necessary," said Ballard, finished with tending his rope. "I want some sleep before we ride."

"At dawn," Ogelvie said. He rubbed his hands together. The way the flickering light from the fire caught his high cheekbones and gaunt face reminded Slocum of a drawing he'd seen once. It had been a sketch of the Grim Reaper.

The first fingers of light from a new day came too soon for Slocum's liking. Ogelvie had already risen and poked the others into action. He wanted to get on the road into Nogales and on to the robbery. Slocum stretched and watched the thin man whip himself into a frenzy. He had seen men do this before, back during the war. In a way, he did it himself, to get ready to meet any unexpected challenge.

In Ogelvie's case, it appeared that the man was getting himself up into a mood to kill.

"Let's ride!" Ogelvie called. "I want to be at their front door the instant they open. We're gonna get rich today, amigos!"

Slocum checked his ebony-handled Colt and found it ready for action, a death-dealing charge loaded into each chamber. On impulse he checked the Winchester rifle sheathed at his saddle. He had the gut feeling it was going to be a long, hard day.

The four men rode into Nogales from the north. The sleepy border town was just beginning to stir. Slocum reached across and pulled the leather thong off the hammer on his Colt. He wanted to be ready when they sighted the bank.

"There she is, boys," said Ogelvie. The man's voice quivered, as if he had just seen the most beautiful woman in the world. "Ballard, you and Delling got the bags?"

"All set," the man answered. He held up a pair of burlap bags. With Lady Luck on their side, the two bags would be stuffed full of greenbacks within a few minutes. They lifted bandannas across their faces and cinched them tight.

"There're a lot of horses tethered outside," muttered Delling as he fumbled with his mask. "Shouldn't we check out what's going on inside before we bust in?"

Slocum was about to second the man's call for caution when Ogelvie let out a rebel yell and spurred his horse onto the rickety boardwalk outside the bank. The clatter of hooves echoed through the peaceful town louder than any cannon fire.

"Get your asses in there!" Ogelvie cried. "If'n you don't, all the money's gonna be mine!"

Ballard hit the ground running. He kicked in the front door with a clatter and swung his pistol around to cover any early-morning customers. Ogelvie pushed in next to him, a scattergun clutched in his hands.

Slocum started to push past Ogelvie when the man cut loose with the shotgun. The roar was quickly drowned out by the agonized cries of wounded men inside the bank.

"There was no call to do that," protested Delling. "They was raising their hands. They knew we was robbin' the damned bank!"

"Shut up," Ogelvie said, stepping over a body and into the bank lobby. He fired a second barrel and threw the shotgun aside, using his six-shooter to cover the rest. "Fork over your valuables, gents, or you'll get another taste of hot lead!"

Ballard began moving among the men, taking watches, wallets, and even two small pokes of gold dust.

"Go on," Slocum said quietly to Delling. The plump man stood frozen by the door, staring at the body on the floor. Toward the back of the bank two others whimpered in pain from the buckshot they'd taken from Ogelvie's weapon.

"I don't know about this," Delling started. He glanced from Slocum to Ogelvie and saw the thin man's hot eyes boring into him. He moved as if he'd been poked with a branding iron.

Slocum moved to one side to keep the customers in a cross-fire between him and Ogelvie. He didn't have to say anything. It was his job to make certain nobody turned into a hero.

"You gettin' anything back there, Delling?" Ogelvie called out. Slocum cursed under his breath. Ogelvie didn't have good sense. The smell of money was making him careless—unless he didn't intend to leave any witnesses.

Slocum made a quick count. One dead already. The three men in front of the counter had turned pale. They read Ogelvie the same way he did. That was bad. They might decide it was better to die trying to save themselves than to let the outlaw slaughter them like sheep. From behind the counter came sounds of two tellers protesting the need to turn over the contents of their cash drawers to Delling.

"Just shoot the sons-a-bitches," growled Ogelvie. "Don't take shit off them!"

"Stay calm," Slocum said to the three customers. "You're going to let us get out of here. You'll be poorer but you'll have stories to tell the grandchildren." Two of them were reassured that they weren't going to lose anything more than their money. The third one scowled at Slocum, as if trying to penetrate the veil of his dirty blue-checked bandanna.

On impulse, Slocum moved closer and pushed the man's canvas duster back. On his chest gleamed a shiny silver star.

"Son of a bitch, a deputy sheriff," crowed Ogelvie. "I ain't killed me a deputy sheriff in *weeks*!"

"And you're not going to now," Slocum said, stepping behind Ogelvie. The man had to face either the deputy or Slocum. Ogelvie got the idea that Slocum was just as likely to back-shoot him as not.

"What's got into you, Slo—"

Slocum fired his Colt Navy to cover Ogelvie's use of his name. It was one thing letting the thin robber call out to Delling. It was another letting him brand John Slocum publicly for bank robbery. Slocum had enough wanted posters following him across the West. He didn't need to be hunted down for still another crime. Yuma Prison wasn't a spot where he wanted to spend any time.

Not for the likes of Ogelvie.

"Don't kill him unless you have to," Slocum said in his cold voice.

"What if I *want* to put him into a shallow grave? I don't *like* deputy sheriffs."

"Got the money?" Slocum shouted at Ballard and Delling. Both men held up their burlap bags. Neither carried the amount of money he had hoped for. "Let's get out of here." Slocum cast a quick look at the deputy sheriff to make sure he wasn't going to do anything foolish.

Ogelvie hesitated, his finger white around the trigger of his six-shooter. Slocum pushed the man into the street and snarled, "Don't make trouble for us. They'll have a posse on our tail inside a few minutes if you shoot him."

"They will anyway. We shoulda kilt the whole damned lot of them," snapped Ogelvie. The scrawny man swung onto horseback and put his heels into the flanks of his horse. The large stallion reared at the sudden pain from Ogelvie's spurs. The man displayed more strength than sense getting the horse back into the street and under control.

By the time Ogelvie started shooting, Slocum and the others were at the southern limits of Nogales.

"Ain't got a lick of sense," grumbled Ballard. "We

should never have throwed in with the likes of Sam Ogelvie."

Slocum snorted. He had never heard Ogelvie's first name before this. Knowing it did nothing to make him like the man any more. He pulled down the brim of his battered brown Stetson and concentrated on riding due south. They could make Mexico before the deputy got a good-sized posse together.

"We didn't get all that much, Slocum," panted Delling. "I knew this was a mistake. We risked our necks and didn't get jack shit!"

Slocum didn't bother replying. It was like this too much of the time. They'd needed four men to rob the bank. It was unfortunate that one of them had to be Sam Ogelvie. For that matter, Slocum wasn't much taken with either of the remaining two men. Ballard and Delling weren't prime candidates for staying out of prison. They both panicked too easily.

From behind Slocum heard the pounding of hooves. He glanced back over his shoulder at the powerful stallion overtaking them. Gobs of white foam flecked the beast, and its eyes were wild. He couldn't tell, but it looked as if blood dripped from the animal's abused flanks where Ogelvie's cruel spurs continually raked.

"Slow up," shouted Slocum. "We're going to kill the horses if we keep up this pace." He reined back and saw that Ballard and Delling did as he ordered. Ogelvie raced on by, then wheeled and came back toward them. The man had finally remembered who was carrying the loot from the robbery.

"How much did we make?" Ogelvie demanded. He started to dismount when Slocum held up his hand as a tacit request for silence. Straining hard, he thought he heard sounds of pursuit. Slocum looked around and pointed toward a low hill.

"Let's split the take there," he said. "There's someone on the trail behind us."

"Couldn't be," scoffed Ogelvie. "We got in and out of Nogales too fast for any posse to form. They're still holding their—" He fell silent when he saw the cloud of dust forming behind them.

"How the hell did they get a posse together *this* fast?" wondered Ballard. "I seen 'em have to wire to Washington for special funds to pay a posse. We shoulda been in Mexico before they even got a reply."

"There are at least ten men after us," said Slocum, judging from the dust cloud the number of riders approaching. "Maybe more. We might have crossed the wrong man."

"What do you mean?" asked Ogelvie. He fingered the six-shooter in his holster, obviously itching for a fight. Slocum wasn't inclined to give the posse the chance to shoot it out with them. Running was better than dying any day.

"It might be an Arizona Ranger named Buck Johnson. I heard tell he was patrolling the southern part of the state this month. If it is him, we've got a world of trouble on our hands. He doesn't give up when he gets on a scent. Ever."

"Sounds as if you and this Buck Johnson have more'n a passing acquaintance," said Ogelvie.

"We've met," Slocum said, not wanting to go into it. He and Johnson had locked horns twice before. Only having a faster horse had kept him out of the Arizona Ranger's clutches.

"We can get to the high ground and stand 'em off," said Ogelvie, still hankering for a fight.

"Like hell we can fight an entire posse! We ride for the border and hope they don't catch us," said Delling. The plump man's face was beaded with sweat. The settling dust had caked in places, giving him the appearance of a dirt farmer who'd been in the fields all day and was ready for a rest.

"Delling's right," said Slocum. "We can't fight the entire Arizona Rangers."

"Ain't but one or two of 'em in these parts," said Ogelvie. "The rest is just a posse. They'll turn tail and run at the first gunshot."

"No," started Delling.

"Shut up," Slocum said dispassionately to the small man. He swung around and stared hard into Ogelvie's eyes. The wildness was there—and it had turned to kill-crazy. He might do them all a passel of good by just shooting Ogelvie like the mad dog he was becoming.

"Let's discuss this off the road," Ballard said nervously. "Those boys are getting real close."

Slocum herded the others ahead of him off the road, got down, and grabbed a low-growing greasewood bush. He tugged but couldn't get it out of the ground. Its long roots sank down dozens of feet into the sun-baked dirt, looking for life-giving water. A whir of lariat made Slocum step back. Ballard's rope settled easily around the bush. The man's horse backed up slowly and pulled the green shrub out. Ballard smiled crookedly and indicated that he knew what to do. Slocum mounted and followed Delling and Ogelvie. Ballard brought up the rear, dragging the bush to hide their tracks in the dry, crusty sand. It wouldn't put a good tracker off for long, but it might give them a few added minutes.

Slocum knew that if Buck Johnson was on his trail, even a few minutes might mean the difference between life and death. Johnson had a reputation of always catching his quarry but seldom bringing them back alive.

"Damnation, Slocum, you was right. Look at that!" cried Delling. The portly man handed over a small brass-encased spyglass he'd pulled out of his bedroll. Slocum hadn't even known the man carried it.

Slocum lifted the spyglass to his right eye and worked for a few seconds to get the posse into the narrow field of vision. The first thing he saw was the Arizona Ranger star gleaming on the lead rider's chest. He let the image bob around a mite, then worked up and focused on the Ranger's face.

"It's Buck Johnson, all right," he said, lowering the glass. "He rode on by where we left the trail, but he'll be back. We don't have more than a few minutes."

"Let's make a stand," insisted Ogelvie.

"Let's divvy up the take and go our separate ways," said Ballard. "I don't much cotton to the notion of this here Buck Johnson coming after me."

Slocum hefted the spyglass again. He went cold inside. "We'd better ride for the border," he said. "The Ranger's found our trail. He's not five minutes behind us!"

2

"I want my share now!" cried Sam Ogelvie. "Don't you go tryin' to ride off with what's rightly mine, you mangy cayuse." He brandished his six-shooter at Ballard. The man's face turned pale when he saw that Ogelvie was trying to wheel his balking stallion around to get a good shot at him.

"Stop it," snapped Slocum. He handed the spyglass back to Delling. The plump man's hands shook as he lifted it to stare at the rapidly approaching Arizona Ranger and his posse. "We've got to split up. That's the only way any of us will get out of this alive. There are too many of them to fight, damn it."

Even Ogelvie had to admit Slocum was right.

"There's no time to split the money properly," Slocum went on. "Ballard, give your sack to Delling." Ballard willingly tossed it across to the frightened Delling.

"What do I do with it?" Delling asked, his voice almost cracking with strain.

"You keep it," Slocum said coldly, "until we join up again in four days. South of the border. The narrow-gauge railroads cross at Hermosilla. We'll divvy up the take then." He looked from Ogelvie to Ballard and back. "There's no problem letting Delling keep the money until then, is there?"

Ogelvie laughed harshly. "He's too chickenshit to cross us. He'll do." Ogelvie spurred his horse viciously and caused it to rear. "In four days, asshole. Be there!" With that warning, he raced down the low hill and across the Sonora Desert, heading west.

"I won't double-cross you, honest," said Delling.

"Just be there. And don't let Buck Johnson catch you. He's as likely to hang you from a cottonwood as he is to take you back to Nogales to stand trial." Slocum saw that the Arizona Ranger had increased his speed now that he had the scent. Like a hound dog on a trail, he would never quit until he spilled blood. Slocum smiled to himself. The Ranger wasn't doing his horse any favors pushing it this hard. It would die under him in another mile if he kept up the hard gallop.

Slocum looked around. Ballard and Delling had already followed Ogelvie down the sandy hillside. Slocum took off after them, letting his tracks mingle with the others until he got to the bottom of the knoll. He had almost ten minutes before Johnson reached the low summit and caught sight of his fugitives. It wasn't long, but Slocum intended to make it do.

He trotted briskly, not wanting to tire his horse yet. The sand varied from having a hard crust almost like a roadbed to treacherously soft and shifting. When he heard a rifle firing, he turned and looked back, fearing that the Ranger had somehow caught up. He need not have worried. Buck Johnson stood on the crest where Slocum and the others had parted company and shook his fist at the sky. Who had fired, Slocum couldn't say, but the range was too great for him to worry over. Slocum wasn't even sure Johnson had spotted him. He could be venting his wrath at having missed them or in seeing one of the others and being unable to pursue immediately.

Everyone had problems. The more troubles he could give Buck Johnson the fewer he'd have during his escape. Slocum turned his horse south toward Mexico. He didn't think he could go directly into the country, but he wanted to make it look as if this was his intent. Another hour's riding convinced him that the posse had taken out after someone else. He hoped it was Ogelvie. The man was nothing but trouble and would become even less manageable when they got to Hermosilla and found that the take from the robbery wasn't as rich as they'd hoped. For Slocum, this was a fact of life. For Ogelvie, it might mean lead starting to fly.

Slocum shrugged off this future problem. He had learned to deal with one day at a time ever since the end of the war. He had returned to the family farm in Calhoun, Georgia, his parents dead and his brother Robert killed during that damnfool Pickett's Charge.

Slocum touched the watch riding high in a vest pocket. This was all he had to remind him of his brother. For the few months he'd spent at the farm, he had a lifetime of woe trailing him.

A carpetbagger judge had taken a shine to the land and thought it would make a good stud farm. When the Reconstruction judge and his hired gunman showed up to take the property from Slocum, "for not payin' back taxes owed throughout the war," he hadn't thought he would find any trouble.

Slocum had ridden with Quantrill and his bloody-handed butchers in Kansas for almost two years. Their wanton killing had sickened him, but he'd been one of them and had done his share of murdering. Killing a thieving Northern judge and a too-slow gunman hardly nudged his conscience after all he'd seen and done in the name of war. He had left two new graves on the hill up by the springhouse when he rode out the next morning.

But judge-killing was a serious crime, and the wanted posters had followed Slocum through the West like flypaper stuck on his boot sole. Even ten years after the crime, the echoes still rang in his ears.

He wasn't going to let Buck Johnson or the posse catch him and find the yellowed poster in some forgotten file cabinet.

After another hour of riding, he cut due east and rode a few miles, then angled toward the south and east. He was never quite sure when he entered Mexico; the desert didn't change appearance. Here and there he saw the tall, long-armed saguaros that grew only in the Sonora Desert. Creosote brush and mesquite trees grew in profusion along long-dry arroyos, and here and there he saw the red-tipped spiny whips of the ocotillo. The Spanish bayonets told him more than anything else he was pushing farther south and into Mexico. He had to keep his horse from stepping on the slender green blade with the impossibly sharp tip. A single accident could cripple a horse—or a man.

Slocum found a rocky arroyo to spend the night, his cooking fire hidden by the tall bank. The next day he rode hard due south and eventually crossed the narrow-gauge railroad line from Nogales. At the sight of the train tracks, he smiled. He had eluded the posse. All that remained was to make his way deeper into the Mexican interior and get to Hermosilla.

"Delling will be there," he said aloud. "That man took off like a stepped-on cat. No Arizona Ranger is going to catch him." About Ballard's skill in eluding the posse, he had no idea. The man had never said much, and Slocum had never formed much of an opinion about him as a man or about his abilities.

Sam Ogelvie was another matter. Slocum wished him nothing but ill luck. He would have murdered everyone in the Nogales bank if Slocum hadn't stopped him.

Killing because it was necessary didn't bother Slocum. Pointless slaughter did.

The loud, long hoot of a train whistle caused Slocum to rein in. He leaned forward, curling his left leg around the pommel. Muscles stretched, and he groaned slightly. Riding his hard had taken its toll on him and his paint horse. He idly thought of flagging down the train and riding into Hermosilla in style. The train rattled by a couple hundred yards away, pulling three passenger cars and two mail cars. In the caboose he saw the silhouettes of two men facing one another, probably playing cards to while away the time to Hermosilla.

He watched the train rattle along its rusted tracks and decided to continue on, living off the land and not taking the easy way into the sleepy interior town. From Hermosilla he could take his cut of the money and go on down to Guaymas or catch the Pacific train and wander back up to California as he'd intended before the robbery.

All that mattered was escaping the Arizona Ranger. The longer Slocum took to make his way back into U.S. territory, the less likely Buck Johnson was to be on his trail. John Slocum wasn't the only outlaw to be caught. Slocum snorted. By now there were probably a dozen new crimes to keep Buck Johnson occupied.

Two more days passed, and the nature of the land changed slowly. The Sonora River turned the arid landscape into farming country. The pungent odors of hay growing and beans cooking made Slocum's nose wrinkle. He crossed the meandering railroad tracks a final time and sighted Hermosilla. The small town spread out over more of the countryside than he'd thought. It had been years since he'd been down in Mexico, and then he'd never been this far to the west. Rustling cattle along the Texas-Mexico border had afforded him numerous opportunities to slip into the country.

"A town this size ought to have at least one decent saloon," he decided. He patted his paint on her neck and guided the sturdy horse down into the town.

He rode slowly along the dusty main street. The railroad depot was at the other side of town. At the northern end he saw nothing but peons actively pursuing their afternoon siesta. Even though the people he saw were all sleeping, he had the eerie feeling of eyes watching as he passed through.

He saw a small cantina and dismounted. He hitched his horse to a post on the east side, giving the animal a hint of shade. Slocum went inside, the cool dim interior alive with the smell of spilled beer and unwashed bodies.

Glancing around, he saw several Mexicans seated with their backs to the adobe walls, hands around mugs of hot beer. More than one moved to put a hand under the table where he sat. Slocum could almost hear the sound of six-shooters cocking. He ignored the threat posed by half of the men in the cantina opening fire on him.

At the crude bar, he settled his right foot against a bent brass rail and asked for a beer.

"*Cerveza*, eh?" the barkeep acknowledged. "You want to try some tequila? I have special bottle *con gusano*, eh?" When he saw Slocum wasn't interested in the gut-searing liquor, he put a frothing glass of warm beer in front of Slocum. "*Un peso.*"

"Not worth it," Slocum said, pushing it back. "Not more than *veinte centavos*. Twenty centavos."

The bartender smiled and revealed twin rows of perfect white teeth. He shrugged as if saying it was only business. Slocum dropped a U.S. nickel on the bar, which vanished quickly. A pile of small coins came back in change. Slocum paid them scant attention. He didn't want the virtually worthless Mexican money in his pockets.

"You are looking for friends, eh?" asked the barkeep.

Slocum looked at him sharply. "What do you know of

my friends?" Slocum didn't like this. He figured on looking for Ogelvie and the others for a day or more. Some of them might not even make it to Hermosilla until a week had passed. The first cantina he stopped in to take the edge off his desert-created thirst offered pay dirt.

"They are three, and they look for a man described to be one such as yourself," the barkeep said. "The tall one, the mean one, he looks for you especially."

"Do they have names?"

The barkeep shrugged expressively. "In Hermosilla, what good are *norteamericano* names?"

"How long have they been waiting for me?" Slocum asked, still cautious. He turned and glanced around the dimly lit room. Smoke hung in the air and veiled those at the back of the cantina. He tried to hold back the increasing tenseness he felt. Something was wrong, and he couldn't put his finger on it.

"They just arrive, all together this morning."

"On the train?" he asked.

"But of course, on the train. They come from Nogales. Why should they ride across bad country when they can ride in style, eh?"

"They tell you about me?"

The bartender looked at Slocum again. The feral gleam in the man's dark eyes was unmistakable. This as much as anything else put Slocum on his guard.

"The tall one, he mention that another *norteamericano* would be coming through soon. Who else but you, señor?"

"Who else?" muttered Slocum. Louder, he asked, "Where are they? The others who are looking for me?"

The barkeep sneered slightly. "They choose to drink at Miguel's cantina. It is across the street and down a few paces. It is not far, but it is also not so good a place to drink. Another *cerveza*, eh?" The bartender tapped the side of Slocum's half-finished beer. The bitterness did more to kill his desire for more than anything else.

"I'll keep working on this one for a few minutes. Did they say when they wanted to see me?"

"*Sí*, yes, señor. Anytime, the tall one say. He will greet you like long-lost brother."

Slocum dropped a silver dollar onto the stained bar and let it roll around. The ringing of the cartwheel held everyone's attention. "There's more than you're telling me. What is it?"

"I do not think the tall one likes you much," the barkeep said, his eyes on the shiny dollar. It might be more money than he'd seen in a month in this dingy cantina.

"So?"

"So it might be wise to not go too boldly, eh?"

"I've heard that is wise at a place like Miguel's," Slocum said. He left the rest of his beer and the silver dollar on the counter. Before he reached the serape doubling as a door, he knew the silver dollar had vanished, as had the remainder of his beer. He paused, then pushed out into the bright sunlight.

In a town like this, Ogelvie already knew he had arrived. No one had left this cantina since Slocum went in, but the grapevine was fast. Dozens had seen him ride into town. Any of the unseen watchers could have alerted the others.

A crudely lettered sign dangling from one corner of a bracket showed Slocum where the other cantina was. But he didn't see any horses around it. Ballard, Delling, and Ogelvie might have ridden the train into town, but they weren't going to stay on foot long. Slocum frowned. Thinking on it, he couldn't see Ogelvie giving up that large stallion of his, unless it was necessary.

He walked around the side of the cantina and checked his Winchester. The magazine was full. On impulse, he checked the Colt Navy slung in its cross-draw holster and loaded the sixth cylinder, which he kept empty while on the trail. He wanted the hammer resting on an empty cylinder if he happened to strike the pistol accidentally. Now he wanted the extra firepower all six chambers afforded.

Only when he felt he was ready to meet Ogelvie face to face did he mount and ride slowly toward Miguel's cantina. Slocum's cold green eyes slowly surveyed the surrounding buildings. Most were tumbledown adobe with poorly repaired roofs and slits for windows. The walls were thick, some of them three feet and more. That made for adequate protection in a fight but left something to be desired for taking the battle to anyone outside.

Slocum reined back and studied the sign slowly swinging to and fro in the hot Sonoran wind. The sun beat down unmercifully on him. He turned up his collar to protect his neck as he took off his bandanna and wrung it out. The sweat dripped onto the ground and formed tiny islands of mud. Slocum took his time putting the bandanna back on. The tension grew so thick he could almost taste it.

"Amigo," he called out when he saw a man peering out from inside the cantina, "tell Ogelvie I'm here."

The man vanished back into the darkness of the cantina. Inside Slocum heard rustling. The sound of a six-shooter cocking caused Slocum to duck forward over the neck of his mount. The horse bucked and tried to run. Slocum held the paint down.

The bullet blowing away a portion of the thick adobe wall came from behind. Slocum slid off his horse and used the animal's bulk as a shield until he could find where the shot had come from. From atop an adjoining building he saw the glint of sunlight off a blued rifle barrel.

Slocum jerked his own rifle from its sheath. Resting the barrel across his saddle, he squeezed off a shot. The horse bucked and tried to run. He kept it under control.

"Drop the rifle or you're buzzard bait," came a cold voice from behind.

Slocum looked over his shoulder and saw Buck Johnson in the doorway to the cantina. He had six-shooters in each hand. The top of the Arizona Ranger's head brushed the lintel. Slocum cursed his oversight. The bartender in the other cantina had said a tall *norteamericano* waited for him here. Slocum had assumed the barkeep had meant Sam Ogelvie.

He'd forgotten just how tall Buck Johnson was.

"Good-bye," the Ranger said, both pistols coming up to gun down Slocum.

"No need," said Slocum. He dropped his rifle and turned. As he did so, he elbowed his skittish horse. The paint reared. In that instant, Slocum went for his Colt Navy. No pistol was more accurate or got off a first shot faster.

Even so, he was drawing against a wary opponent with two pistols already trained on their target. Slocum saw a red blossom grow on the Arizona Ranger's right side. Then everything was obscured by twin clouds of gunsmoke from Johnson's pistols.

Fiery lead tore through John Slocum's upper body. He doubled over in pain, and the hot desert sand became even hotter when his face pressed into it.

3

Slocum fought hard to keep from blacking out. He spat. Grit stayed on his dried lips. He didn't have enough spit to clear his mouth. He rolled to one side and immediately regretted it. Lances of fire drove mercilessly into his chest. Through red veils of pain he saw Buck Johnson wobbling in the cantina doorway. The hot desert wind had blown away the heavy clouds of choking smoke from his black-powder pistols.

Slocum fought against a six-shooter turned to lead in his hand. Struggling, he lifted it and squeezed off a shot. The Arizona Ranger's hat flew off his head and back into the cantina. More than this, Slocum saw a red crease open on the man's forehead. Johnson's knees buckled, and he fell bonelessly to the ground. Slocum didn't know if the man was dead and didn't much care. He hurt too much and had to get out of town. There was still at least one more lawman in town who wanted his hide.

Left arm across his chest, trying to hold himself together, Slocum got to his feet. The world spun in wide, wild circles around his head. Dizziness caught him in its treacherous web and almost cast him back to the dusty ground. He threw his right arm over his saddle.

Another shot rang out. The man with the rifle on the adobe next door had seen what had happened and had started firing again. Slocum's eyesight was too blurred to find the man. He started to fetch his fallen rifle and quickly realized that he couldn't.

If he tried, he'd fall over and never stand up again. Using what seemed to be his last ounce of strength, Slocum slid into the saddle and put his heels to the paint's flanks. For the first time he wished he had Ogelvie's cruel spurs. He needed to put as much distance between Hermosilla and himself as possible.

Another shot came close to plucking him out of the saddle. The hot streak across his back rivaled the burning pits in his chest. Then he was out of town and racing to . . . where? Slocum neither knew nor cared. He had escaped Buck Johnson's trap. Nothing else mattered. Nothing.

Warm darkness closed around him, squeezing down hard until he passed out.

The two chest wounds didn't bleed much, but Slocum knew the slugs were inside, festering, gnawing away at him, turning his guts to rotted meat. He pulled out the thick-bladed knife he always carried in a sheath at the small of his back and started to dig out the slug in his left shoulder. Weakness washed over him like a warm ocean surf. He passed out, to come to again an hour later.

Hand shaking he sheathed the knife. He wasn't up to operating on himself. He was too weak.

And new sounds came to him in his hiding spot.

"Damnation," Slocum muttered. He forced himself erect and stared back across the arid Sonoran sand dunes. His worst nightmare had just come true.

Buck Johnson was on his trail.

"That man must be the devil himself." Slocum felt

better than he had before he passed out, but he wasn't up to a shoot-out with the Arizona Ranger. If he fought anything stronger than a newborn kitten, he was likely to lose.

Slocum studied the way the Ranger rode and knew he *had* hit the lawman back in Hermosilla. Johnson's right arm didn't move; as he turned in the saddle Slocum saw that the man had it in a sling. A sudden glint of sunlight off the Ranger's forehead showed white plaster where someone had patched the head wound. Buck Johnson wasn't in perfect shape, but he was a damn sight better off than Slocum. Of the Arizona Ranger's backup Slocum saw no trace.

That worried him. If they had split up, Slocum knew he might be turning from the Ranger and running straight into another ambush. Slocum hunkered down and tried to conserve his strength. He worked out all that had happened back in Hermosilla and didn't like it one bit.

Had Delling sold him out? Or had Johnson caught him or Ballard and tortured the information about their meeting place from him? Slocum knew the Ranger wasn't a kind interrogator. The fact was, Buck Johnson made some of the Mescalero Apache braves look down-right tame and peaceable by comparison.

Whatever had happened had gone quick back in Arizona. The Ranger and his deputy had ridden down on the train from Nogales to Hermosilla to beat Slocum there by a day or more. Slocum shuddered. He had seen the train rattling by out in the middle of the desert and had thought about flagging it down for a ride. That might have been the very train Buck Johnson had taken.

Slocum moaned softly as new waves of pain flooded his body. Maybe it would have been better to have it out with the Arizona Ranger on the train rather than in town. It would have been over a couple of days earlier. Slocum cursed the man's diligence and his ignoring the Mexican border the way he did. No U.S. territory lawman was supposed to cross over in hot pursuit. The Congress and the Mexican president had decided this wasn't in the best interests of either country.

But Buck Johnson wasn't beholden to either a Congress back in Washington or a Mexican bureaucrat over in the middle of the swamp surrounding Mexico City.

Heaving himself up and into his saddle, Slocum knew he had to ride. If he stayed, he died. He might anyway, but he wanted to go down fighting. He had almost taken Buck Johnson once. He might get the chance again—if he kept moving and didn't make a direct stand.

Slocum cursed the lack of a rifle now. During the war he had been a sniper for the Confederacy. More than one battle had gone the rebel way because of Slocum's sharpshooting. Finding the sunlight glinting off a Union officer's braid was easy. It was almost as easy sighting down the long rifle barrel and squeezing off the shot that robbed the Northern forces of their leaders.

His Colt Navy was a fine weapon, but it wasn't up to the long-distance shooting necessary to take Buck Johnson out of the saddle permanently.

Slocum cut back toward the west, zigzagging as he rode to give the Ranger as hard a chase as possible. It took its toll on Slocum, but he had no other choice. When he crossed the railroad tracks leading south toward Guaymas he knew he wasn't going to get away from the Ranger. His entire body ached and he was faint. He could hardly lift his six-shooter, and firing it accurately might be beyond his strength.

To the east rose tall mountains. The Sierras drew him. He dared not stay out in the flat lands where Johnson could spot him easily. Dodging into the mountains seemed his only hope.

If only the mountains weren't so far off.

For hours, he rode on rocky ground that would cover his tracks. He began to think he could reach the mountains without being gunned down when he saw a cloud of dust to the south and east. From the direction of travel, a large group of riders would intersect his path within the hour. Slocum reined in and frowned. There weren't many companies of men this size likely to be riding at the edge of the Sonoran Desert.

"Federales," he decided. He had ridden from the frying pan straight into the fire. The Mexican national police weren't likely to let a lone gringo rider go on his way in peace. If anything, they might decide he was a criminal and take him in—or just hang him for the hell of it. Slocum had heard of them doing worse than that.

If Buck Johnson represented the worst of American law, the Federales put a new twist to it with a vicious disregard for life.

Federales or Arizona Ranger. Slocum didn't seem to have much choice. He judged the distance into the mountains and knew he'd never reach them before the Federales caught him. The speed at which they were riding spoke of urgency. They might have spotted him, or they might just be out for a day's patrol. Whatever the reason, Slocum was dead meat if they caught him.

He headed for low foothills. The small canyons and winding passages leading back into the taller Sierras might afford him escape. Slocum bent over his paint's neck and held on for dear life. Getting into those hills meant his life. If he fell off the horse now . . .

Slocum felt rather than heard the bullet pass close to his side. He looked around and saw Buck Johnson behind him. The Arizona Ranger's horse reared and almost threw him. Slocum put his heels into his own horse, but the paint was tired. The animal did the best it could, but Slocum knew the Ranger was going to get him.

From the south came the pounding of dozens of hooves. He didn't have to look that way to know the band of Federales was almost on top of him, too. He was caught between death behind and death to the right.

Ahead lay, at best, temporary escape. But keeping on toward the low hills was all he could do.

More rifle shots from behind showed that Johnson was getting itchy, but none of the slugs came as close as the first had. Slocum began to hope. Maybe the Federales would stop the Ranger. They didn't care for any gringo intruding on their territory. If only he could hang on for a while longer.

Rocky bluffs grew around him, shielding him from view by the Federales. Behind came the relentless Arizona Ranger. Slocum kept his horse moving, even if it wasn't at the breakneck clip he needed right now to escape. He turned up the first branching canyon and headed directly into the mountains. There might be a box canyon to trap him—or worse. He might find himself trapped between the Mexicans and the Arizona Ranger in a rocky draw.

Slocum looked around for a place to make a stand. His trusty Colt wasn't much against his foes, but he had to try. His body refused to accept any more abuse. His shoulders were starting to tighten up on him. And inside he felt liquid squirting around. He needed rest and a doctor.

He wasn't likely to get either.

With any luck, Buck Johnson might consent to bury him on the spot rather than let the buzzards have him for dinner.

Slocum urged his paint up a slope covered with loose pebbles. The horse protested but valiantly obeyed. At the top Slocum found a small indentation in the side of the hill—hardly even a cave, but more protection than staying in the open. He dismounted, tethered his horse to a low jacaranda bush, and drew his six-shooter.

Almost gladly he dropped to the hard ground and peered back down the slope. The support under him felt better than any down-filled mattress. He fought off the lethargy creeping up on him. To pass out now meant death. He had to fight.

His Colt exploded in his hand, jarring him fully awake. He hadn't even realized his finger had curled around the trigger. He had no idea where the slug had gone. This worried Slocum enough to force himself to a sitting position. He was more exposed but was better able to keep alert.

The echo from the shot rattled down the narrow canyon. He cursed his foolishness. Johnson might not be easily fooled into thinking his quarry had escaped, but all chance of that was gone now. The gunshot meant Slocum was somewhere near.

The report died out, replaced by the thunder of hooves. Slocum sighed. He'd been right. This wasn't a canyon as much as it was a shortcut from one side of the hilly formation to the other. The Federales had entered the far side and were now pounding down hard toward him. With the Arizona Ranger in the other direction Slocum found himself caught in the jaws of a giant, deadly animal.

The Mexican soldiers came into view and then slowed. Slocum wished he had his rifle. Buck Johnson rode up slowly to the officer at the front of the Federales' column. Slocum cursed anew. The lawman must have a tongue of the purest liquid silver. Not only didn't the Mexican *comandante* kill the American out of hand, he waved his troops around and toward the spot where Slocum had struggled up the slope.

Arizona Ranger rode next to Federale commander to the base of the hill. Slocum felt the ebony grip turn slippery with his sweat. He didn't have long to live.

"Come on down," called Buck Johnson. "Make it easy on all of us. Captain Gomez doesn't want to risk any of his men going up after you. And I wouldn't want him to," the Ranger added hastily. "I'll come for you myself."

Slocum looked around for some way out. There weren't any rocks large enough for him to pry loose and cause a small avalanche, even if he had the strength. He had five rounds left in his Colt Navy. And he could hardly stand up.

"Come get me," he shouted down the hill. Slocum put his back to the rock and waited.

The Ranger and the Federales' officer spoke for several minutes. Slocum didn't care if they had a falling out. Let them kill one another. That was the only way he could ever escape. Even this impossible dream vanished when he saw Buck Johnson and two of the soldiers begin picking their way up the slope.

Slocum watched and waited for them to come into range of his pistol. Just as he was squeezing back on the trigger, a shot rang out. Again Slocum was startled. But this time he hadn't fired.

The soldier riding to the left of the Arizona Ranger threw his arms into the air and fell backward off his horse. Johnson and the other soldier spun around, looking for the source of the gunfire. A second shot filled the canyon with ear-splitting noise.

Then all hell broke loose. The two shots had been tentative, like a small boy sticking his toe in to test the temperature of the water before plunging into a stock pond. The temperature was good; bullets sang their deadly song and cut down one soldier after another.

Slocum simply stared. The fusillade came from both ends of the narrow, rocky gap. As the Federales and the Ranger had trapped him, so had they become trapped in the jaws of a giant vise. The air filled with the pungent odor of burning gunpowder, and soon a blue-gray pall hung over the canyon.

Slocum dropped back to his belly and wiggled forward. Peering over the brink, he saw Buck Johnson on his hands and knees a hundred yards away. The distance was too great for accurate shooting. Slocum held off. Patience might reward him with a better chance later. Whoever had cut down the Mexican soldiers might decide to remove all witnesses from this bloody battle-field.

The lucky Federales who survived the first attack scrambled for cover. Their rudimentary military training took over, and they put up a better fight than Slocum would have thought possible. When bullets began raining down on them from the canyon rim, they were doomed. To a man they died.

Slocum lay with his head on a rock. He might have passed out again. He wasn't sure. When he noticed activity down below again, he saw no trace of the Arizona Ranger. From both sides came the slow, steady infiltration of a ragtag band of *pistoleros*. Slocum saw the sun shining off crossed bandoliers and rifle barrels as they came to investigate their handiwork.

The silent aftermath worked on Slocum's nerves. He was usually a patient man. His wounds caused him considerable pain, and his hands shook uncontrollably. He wanted something to happen. Anything.

Into the silence of the *pistoleros'* stripping the soldiers' bodies of arms and ammunition and valuables came a tall vaquero riding a white stallion. Occasional glints of gold showed from the man's face. Slocum squinted as he tried to make out details.

"Amigos!" cried the rider. "This is a great day for our cause. The accursed Federales lay dead before us!"

A cheer went up. Slocum wiggled back from the brink and tried to imagine himself turning invisible. There might be as many as two dozen banditos below. They had wiped out a government band sent after them, and they were just as likely willing to kill a gringo who had blundered into their stronghold.

"Up there, on the mountainside. Show yourself!" The *pistolero* on the stallion rode to the foot of the slope. "Show yourself to the *jefe de las sierras*!"

Slocum tried to stand and fell back.

"If you do not obey, we will kill you—slowly!"

Slocum lurched forward and stood on the edge, staring down at the bandito. The golden ray he had seen earlier came from the man's front tooth. It had been capped in solid gold.

"They were after me," Slocum called as loudly as he could. His voice sounded hoarse and tinny. He wondered if the *pistolero* could even hear him.

"No longer do they seek you," cried the man. "They all lie dead at my feet."

Slocum wobbled. He tried to put away his pistol. He wasn't sure if he got it into the soft leather cross-draw holster or not. The world swam in front of his eyes and turned increasingly dark.

"You no longer need fear the Federales," continued the bandit leader. "You need fear only *me*, Jaime Rodriguez!"

4

John Slocum awoke to a world of new pain. He looked up and saw only wisps of high, thin ice clouds floating above. Then a heavy darkness descended over him. He forced himself to concentrate. From the dark cloud shone a ray of the purest gold.

He tried to reach for his trusty six-shooter. He wasn't sure if Jaime Rodriguez was preventing him from drawing his pistol or if he was paralyzed.

"Amigo, you are once more among the living. *Bueno!*"

"You didn't kill me?"

"What a question! But of course not! You are hunted by the Federales. That means you are a friend to us. You and I are friends, no?"

"Yes," Slocum got out feebly. Weakness assailed him again. He felt sick to his stomach, and his chest burned like all the prairie fires ever lit by the Comanches.

Slocum tried to keep awake but couldn't. The bouncing drove blistering spikes into his shoulders where the Ranger's bullets had penetrated. Inside he felt liquid welling up. He was bleeding, but it didn't show. He was dying and knew it.

When he came to again it was to pain he had never realized existed. Jaime Rodriguez stood over him, a grim expression on his swarthy face. The *pistolero* was shaking his head. Slocum tried to pull away from the pain and failed. As he turned he caught the whiff of something—perfume?

He doubted his senses. These mountain bandits weren't inclined to use rose-scented toilet water. Slocum blinked. The hands working on his left shoulder were smaller than those of the *pistolero*. Smaller, finer, and unaccustomed to the labor that must go with living in a bandit camp.

"Who?" he asked.

"Hush," came a soft, sibilant voice. "I am Consuela. You will be all right. These bullets are going to make you very sick unless I remove them both."

Slocum felt a new searing pain and passed out. But this time visions of angels danced in his head.

Slocum sipped the warm chicken broth from the decorated pottery bowl Consuela held. The salty tang bit into his lips and tongue. He drank quickly, surprised at how famished he was.

"Not so fast," she laughed. When she spoke it sounded like silver bells chiming. Slocum was captivated by her voice and wild beauty. Long black hair had been tossed behind her and caught up with a clip inset with turquoise. High cheekbones and full, lush red lips invited him to do more than look. But her eyes held him captive.

Dark brown pools sucked him into the center of her very soul. He wondered if he could get lost in them—and he started wondering if he wanted to.

"I don't remember too much," Slocum admitted. "I remember Rodriguez calling to me that I had to fear him, then there wasn't much but pain." His green eyes fixed on her. "And I remember seeing you. I thought it was a fever dream."

"I fixed the wounds in your shoulders. They still do not heal properly. You rode far with those bullets in you?"

"I don't know how far," he said. "It happened in Hermosilla."

"So far!" she cried. "You are truly a man of great strength and resolve to endure such agony over such a distance."

"I didn't have any choice. An Arizona Ranger was hot on my trail."

"Why was that?" she asked. Slocum tensed. Consuela's tone had changed subtly.

"Some friends and I had robbed a bank in Nogales. The Ranger wanted us for that. I don't know how he discovered we were going to meet in Hermosilla."

"Everyone has his price," Consuela said softly.

Slocum started to answer when a shadow fell across his chest. He turned and looked back. Jaime Rodriguez stood listening, hands resting on the butts of two silver-handled revolvers thrust into his belt. Slocum thought his eyes were deceiving him, then saw that Rodriguez was missing the little finger on his right hand.

"You rob banks, eh, amigo?" Rodriguez walked around and stared over Consuela's shoulder.

Slocum grew increasingly uneasy. He had missed something between the bandito leader and the woman. She wasn't any peon off a farm. Consuela had the air of the hacienda about her—the mistress of a hacienda. Slocum couldn't understand how she and Rodriguez fit together.

"I have," Slocum said, answering the question reluctantly. He knew Rodriguez had overheard his confession to Consuela.

"And trains? Do you rob the railroad trains, also?"

"Why?"

"Ah, he answers with questions. I believe he has experience in robbing the trains *and* the banks."

"I've done both," said Slocum. He struggled to sit up. The pain in his bandaged shoulders made him wince. With Consuela helping, he propped himself against a pile of crates. "Why are you so interested?"

"I wondered why the Federales were chasing you."

"They weren't, not until an Arizona Ranger named Buck Johnson put them onto my trail."

"You speak ill of this man. I hear it in your voice. You do not like him?"

"He chased me into Mexico," said Slocum. "He violated the sovereignty of your country trying to arrest me."

"*Sí,* yes, this is *my* country. What do they know in far-off Mexico City about governing? Do they understand our needs in Sonora when they are in Vera Cruz? Can Lerdo de Terjada know our plight in the Bacatete Mountains? No! He is too busy making his alliances with that *pendejo* Díaz! Where is Juárez now that we need him!"

"Benito is dead," Consuela said softly. Slocum looked at the woman and tried to decipher what she meant by those simple words. She didn't sound as if this suited her, yet at the same time Consuela made it sound as if the great liberator of Mexico was no friend of hers. This added to Slocum's conviction that she was the daughter of a wealthy *patrón*. Juárez had few allies among the property owners who had seen in the poor campesino the seeds of bloody revolution and the loss of their land holdings.

"We will not allow them to carry on. Díaz is the true threat to this country," declared Rodriguez.

"What's this got to do with robbing trains?" asked Slocum.

"Everything!" Rodriguez cried with passion. "We

steal from them to make ourselves stronger. Every peso they lose is our gain."

"And you want to make sure it's doubly your gain by stealing as much gold as you can from the government shipments." Slocum didn't know how Jaime Rodriguez differed from any other bandito in the interior mountains of Mexico, but Rodriguez *had* saved his life. He and Consuela.

"You are a very intelligent man, Señor . . ."

"Slocum. John Slocum."

He felt Consuela's hand slowly working up and down his arm. Wherever she touched his flesh it turned warm.

"We can work together for our mutual benefit, no?"

"I don't see how I can get anything out of any deal," Slocum said. "You're not offering to split any take if we go into robbing trains."

Rodriguez laughed heartily. He covered his mouth with his right hand. The lack of a little finger let the gold tooth show through easily, giving him a barbaric look.

"You have the sense of humor that is so rare among gringos. Of course you get no gold from our robberies. But we can trade, you and I. We can deal as professionals."

"I don't have anything you'd want." Slocum knew the *pistolero* could have stolen all his belongings while he was unconscious. For all that, Rodriguez could have left him to die among the fallen Federales.

"Jaime has tried robbing the government gold shipments. There are always too many Federales guarding it. We need assistance."

"You want someone to plan the robbery for you?"

"It is well known that north of the border the gold trains are guarded by hundreds of your U.S. Cavalry. Yet robbery is common. How do you get around so many soldiers?"

Slocum almost laughed. Then he saw the bandit leader was serious. How many times must Rodriguez have tried to rob from the government gold shipments and failed to make such an offer to a gringo? Slocum wasn't sure he wanted to know the answer to that.

"There is always much danger," said Consuela. "Jaime has not told you of the other problems."

"There are the Yaquis," the bandit leader said seriously. "In these Bacatete Mountains are scattered tribes of the *indios*. They have not thought well of any white or Mexican for some time."

"Many fought against the French when they invaded Guaymas in 1865," said Consuela. "They feel betrayed by the reforms which stripped them of their land. The Eight Pueblos are armed camps now."

"Where are they?" asked Slocum. The last thing he wanted was to cross a Yaqui. He had heard stories of their brutality, their fighting prowess, their incredible stamina in battle.

"They watch the trains as they go from Hermosilla to the south," said Rodriguez. "That is one reason there are so many guards on each train."

"You're another reason," Slocum guessed. The *pistolero* smiled broadly, showing once more the gold tooth.

"But of course I am!" he bragged. From the other side of the camp came the sounds of a fight. Rodriguez muttered under his breath and hurried off to quell the minor skirmish.

Consuela watched him go. Slocum tried to figure out what she felt for the man. She seemed out of place in the camp.

"How many other revolutionary bands are out here in these mountains?" he asked. The woman shrugged, as if it were a matter of no consequence to her.

"The Federales," Slocum pressed. "Are there many more of them patrolling the area?"

"You think to escape. You gringos are so easy to see through," she said. She sat on the ground facing him, her legs tucked under her. Slocum reached out and touched the hem of her skirt. The material, now dirty and torn, had once been the finest cotton. She was no camp whore.

"I wish to dress again in fine clothing," Consuela said wistfully. She tried smoothing out the wrinkled, torn dress and finally gave up the attempt to make it into what it had once been.

Slocum held his tongue. He didn't know the woman's status in the camp. From the way she spoke, she was not here voluntarily, yet she didn't seem to be a prisoner either. His own position was more important to him. Slocum didn't want to trade the Arizona Ranger for a Mexican desperado.

"Jaime is a good leader," Consuela said. "He inspires his men, but they lack the training. It is a miracle that they do so well against the Federales."

"They weren't that good," Slocum said. "It took them too long to realize Rodriguez was firing on them."

She shrugged, and Slocum thought the simple gesture was gorgeous. Her bare shoulders poked through the top of the dress. Just below, the flare of her breasts set his heart hammering more fiercely. Consuela had a trim waist and bare legs that perfectly completed an already lovely picture.

Before he could ask about the camp's location, Jaime Rodriguez returned, his knuckles skinned and his face clouded with unrestrained fury.

"Like small children, they fight," he grumbled. "It is all I can do to keep them in line. But I do what I must." His hot, fierce eyes challenged Slocum to argue.

Slocum said nothing.

"You have given some thought to aiding us, eh?" asked the *pistolero*. "We can use a man of your experience. Robbing the trains south of the border cannot be much different from robbing them up north."

"The number of guards is different. Getting away

might be different," Slocum allowed. "What about the Yaquis? Would we have to fight them for the gold?"

"We *always* fight the Yaquis," declared Rodriguez.

"*Sí, siempre,*" Consuela agreed. "They are bitter enemies for control of this region of Mexico. They will learn what it means to be free when Jaime overthrows the tyrants in Mexico City."

"He cares nothing for this," said Rodriguez. "He cares only to rob the trains."

"What do I get out of this?" Slocum asked cautiously. "I wouldn't want any of the gold," he said diplomatically, "since that must all go for your revolution. But my time and skill shouldn't be wasted."

Consuela didn't quite laugh, but the sparkle in her eyes showed her amusement at the way he skirted the issue.

"We get the gold to further the revolution against those in Mexico City," said Rodriguez. "What do you get? You can keep your life."

"That's something," said Slocum. He knew the *pistolero* hadn't kept him alive this long if he wasn't willing to barter. "I might need a bonus for my help. Something to keep me inspired to do the best job possible."

"The Yaquis might like a fine gringo of their own to use as a slave. Some last for many days," said Rodriguez.

Slocum looked at Consuela. She saw he wasn't impressed by the threat. She turned to Rodriguez and parted her lips to speak. The bandit leader caught the small sign and went on smoothly, as if he had only paused for breath.

"We will rid you of the Arizona Ranger."

"Buck Johnson? He's still alive? But I saw him fall at the foot of the hill!" Slocum couldn't believe his ears. There wasn't any way the Ranger could have survived Rodriguez's hail of bullets. He calmed down. Rodriguez was gulling him, trying to get him to respond.

If that was all the desperado wanted, he'd succeeded.

"He leads a charmed life, that one," said the bandit leader. "The Federales all died. He slipped away. When we went through the fallen to . . . check them, he was not among them. Nor did we find a horse outfitted for a gringo."

"I saw him," muttered Slocum. His mind raced. It didn't matter how Johnson had escaped death. He had. And he wouldn't give up as he tracked Slocum down.

"We can help one another, then," said Rodriguez. "You will help us rob the trains, and we will remove this Arizona Ranger from your trail permanently. It is a sad thing to always look over your shoulder waiting for one such as he to catch you, is it not?"

"It is," said Slocum. Consuela turned toward him and smiled just enough to let him know that he'd made the right decision. Again Slocum was confused about her position in the company of bandits.

What didn't confuse him was the promise she so obviously gave him. Robbing trains might be dangerous, but bedding Jaime Rodriguez's woman would be even riskier.

"I'll do what I can," Slocum pledged even as he silently cursed himself for being such a fool.

5

"We outsmart them at every turn!" cried Jaime Rodriguez to his gathered band. "The Federales can do nothing to us. We are strong, and they are weak!"

Slocum kept his cynical view of the bandit leader's speech to himself. The Federales had given Rodriguez hell for the past two weeks, causing him to change his base camp three times. The government soldiers might not be well trained, but they had two powerful goads. Their leaders saw Rodriguez as an affront, if not an outright threat, to their power. And the soldiers had lost comrades-in-arms when Rodriguez had slaughtered the Federale company.

"He speaks well, no?" asked Consuela.

"He keeps his men in line," Slocum said. He looked at the lovely young woman. She remained as much of an enigma as she had when he'd opened his eyes and seen her tending his wounds. Slocum stretched and felt healing muscles protest. He'd be stiff for weeks, but the damage had been repaired. Strangely, what hurt worst of all was the narrow gash across his back from the stray rifle bullet. It itched and made sleeping difficult.

"You do not like him, do you, John?"

"I don't dislike him. I find revolutionaries a bit hard to understand."

"Why is that? You said you fought for the Confederacy. Were they not revolutionaries?"

Slocum shook his head. The war years weren't fit memories. "The South wasn't trying to change things, they were trying to preserve them. What matters in the long run is what's right."

"You do not think Jaime is right in what he does?"

He looked at her carefully, wondering at her interrogation. Her face was expressionless. She'd make a good poker player, he decided. But what did she want from him?

"This isn't my country or my place to make judgments like that," he answered carefully. "I just want to get rid of the Arizona Ranger on my trail."

"Jaime promised. He will stop this Buck Johnson for you. Then you will rob trains together and bring much gold to the cause."

"Is it your cause, too?"

"Women do not have causes," she said with more than a touch of bitterness. "Women do as they are told and nothing more. That is the way it has always been."

Slocum smiled crookedly. "Most of the women I've known would argue that point with you. They were pretty independent."

"Do you have a woman? North of the border?"

"No." Slocum left it at that. Jaime Rodriguez finished his harangue and joined them. His arm snaked around Consuela's shoulders as he pulled her close. Slocum saw a small tensing of the woman's muscles, but she did not try to move away from the bandito.

"They are ready for action, Señor Slocum," Rodriguez said. "They will find your Ranger and finish him for you."

"Good. What about the Federales?"

"Pah! They are nothing. We make fools of them at every turn. They look but do not find. We look—and kill!"

"Fine words," Slocum said. Only Consuela heard the contempt in them. She eyed Slocum with growing interest. Slocum just couldn't decide where Consuela fit into the puzzle of Rodriguez and his ragtag revolutionary army.

"I will rule all Mexico one day soon," declared Rodriguez, squeezing Consuela even tighter. "But we must find your Arizona Ranger and complete our part of the bargain. Are you ready to ride?"

"Now?" This took Slocum by surprise. He thought Rodriguez would demand that he rob a gold shipment before paying off by getting rid of Buck Johnson.

"There is no better time, since my scouts have seen this tall man coming into a box canyon. We know the Bacatete Mountains better than anyone."

"Anyone except the Yaquis," cut in Consuela. Rodriguez was not pleased with her unanticipated comment. That made Slocum believe she cut straight to the truth of the matter. The *indios* ruled these mountains, not Jaime Rodriguez.

"We have him trapped in a box canyon. He cannot escape our swift justice!"

Slocum saddled his paint with some difficulty. The weakness in his arms bothered him, but every day saw improvement. It wouldn't be long before he could slip away from Rodriguez and make for the border. He had some tracking of his own to do in Arizona to find if Delling, Ballard, or Ogelvie—or all of them—had betrayed him to the Ranger.

More than that, he wanted his share of the take from the Nogales bank robbery. He wasn't going to endure being shot up by Johnson and not see a single red cent of the loot.

Slocum settled down in the saddle and waited for

Rodriguez to mount his impressive white charger. The stallion snorted and pawed at the rocky dirt. For all the horse's obvious power and strength, Rodriguez controlled his mount well. He looked the part of a national liberator, a plaza statue of a hero come to life.

"The Federales will not bother us this day," said Rodriguez. "They chase their tails on the other side of the pass. When we have dealt with your problem, we will discuss ways of removing the Federales!" Rodriguez let out a high-pitched yell and waved. Ten men worked to get into a ragged column behind their leader. Slocum rode to one side.

As he left camp, he saw Consuela watching him with her enigmatic dark eyes. He wished he knew more about her, but every time he had turned the conversation to her background, she had avoided it. About all he knew for a fact was that she had done miracles in patching him up.

Just seeing her in camp made him yearn to return.

Slocum settled down and rode to one side of Rodriguez, not wanting to seem to be with him and yet not wanting to stray too far. Whatever else Slocum thought of the prancing peacock of a *pistolero*, Rodriguez knew the Bacatete Mountains better than anyone else in the band. Slocum had watched him sketch out the hidden canyons and passes to his men for them to evade the Federales.

"Come, Señor Slocum, ride beside me," the bandit leader urged. Slocum had little choice but to obey. He was conscious of his lack of standing in the party—and the heavily armed, suspicious men behind him. They had no reason to kill the wily Arizona Ranger other than that they had been told to do it by their leader. For Slocum they would do nothing.

"How far is he?" Slocum asked.

"Always the impatient one, eh?" laughed Rodriguez. "You gringos are alike in many respects. Never rush such things. Let them develop to their fullness. *Then* strike like the rattler!"

"He's tried to kill me more than once. I want to make sure he's out of the way for good before we look over the train schedules and decide which is the best shipment to take," Slocum said, giving the *pistolero* a taste of what he might get if things went according to plan now.

The man's naked greed shone in his chocolate-brown eyes. He wanted more gold than in just his front tooth, Slocum saw. He doubted the man's revolutionary fervor went much deeper than the peon's dream of quick riches.

"We will get him. He cannot escape us now." The man's assurance fell on skeptical ears. Slocum wasn't going to be happy until he dropped the last spadeful of dirt on Buck Johnson's grave.

They rode along the narrow mountain trails until Slocum was too turned around to figure out where they were going. He looked down at the floor of the canyon and saw a small river flowing sluggishly. In the early spring it probably ran from one side of the rocky gorge to the other. Now, in midsummer, it barely held enough to water a horse.

If Slocum had been choosing where to ride, it would have been down there, in the cool shadows, and not on the rocky, hot, dusty trail. But he soon saw what Rodriguez already knew.

Buck Johnson had taken the lower path—and they had the advantage of high ground on him.

"See, Señor Slocum?" The bandito smiled broadly, showing his gold tooth in the afternoon sun. "We have him where we want him. There is no escape back along this canyon. And ahead?"

"What's ahead?" asked Slocum, playing the *pistolero*'s guessing game. He thought he knew the answer.

"A box canyon. There are waterfalls feeding the miserable little stream, but there is no way out. We have him!"

"Why is he down there?" asked Slocum.

Jaime Rodriguez chuckled at his own cleverness. "A false trail. One of my scouts laid it with the greatest of care. Your Ranger follows it to his own death."

Slocum had to admit the plan looked good to him. From their aerial vantage point, the ten men could pick off a rabbit running on the floor of the canyon. The Arizona Ranger had no chance in hell of getting away this time.

Or so it seemed. Slocum still felt uneasy. There ought to be more—and he didn't know what. Too many times the Ranger had eluded him, had escaped death and returned stronger than ever.

"Do you have men on the canyon floor?" Slocum asked.

"There is no need. We are all crack shots, no?" Rodriguez looked behind at the ragtag army with him. They all grinned and muttered among themselves.

"I want to take the first shot," Slocum said. He knew he wouldn't miss. His experience at sniping would stand him in good stead. Buck Johnson would be carrion before the sun went down.

"We shall see, señor, we shall see."

Ten minutes later they came around a rocky prominence and looked down into the box. From where he stood on the precarious brink, Slocum saw a small, green oasis in the canyon. Trees grew, and low shrubs covered the ground with lush vegetation. Twin streams ran down from the heights. And best of all, in the midst of the green stood a tall man wearing a battered brown hat. He knelt down and took off the hat to dip it into a small pond.

"That's him," Slocum said. "He's still got the plaster patch on his forehead where I shot him in Hermosilla."

"So? You wish to try again?" Jaime Rodriguez's tone was taunting. Slocum pulled a rifle from his saddle. He had won it in a poker game with several of the *pistolero*'s lieutenants. They had reluctantly parted with the Winchester, though Slocum was at a loss to know why. Its owner had let it rust. A week's work had gone into polishing away most of the spots and sighting it in.

Even so, Slocum wasn't sure he'd make a clean shot downhill and at this range.

"Have your men get ready, just in case."

"*Sí*, we will be ready."

Slocum jerked around, startled that the bandit leader shouted his commands. The ringing echoes from the order to fire had alerted Buck Johnson. The Ranger jerked to one side, hitting the ground hard and rolling fast.

Slocum cursed. He dropped to one knee, braced his elbow on his knee, and sighted the old rifle as carefully as he could. The distance was considerable, but he thought the Arizona Ranger was just close enough. He fired.

The sharp report rattled through the canyon. Slocum peered through the cloud of gunpowder smoke to see if he'd hit his target.

He couldn't be sure. Buck Johnson lay on the ground, unmoving. But Slocum didn't have the confidence that went with a clean kill. When he fired accurately, it felt *right*. This shot hadn't. He brought the rifle back and got off another shot that dug a tiny pit a foot away from the prone Ranger.

"You are good, Señor Slocum," complimented Rodriguez. "We are better. There are more of our rifles. *Fuera!*"

The reports deafened Slocum. The ten men with Rodriguez fired until their rifles either seized up or their hammers fell on empty chambers. They hooted and hollered as if they'd just won the revolution. Slocum stood and stared down at the body of the Ranger. Buck Johnson still hadn't moved. But Slocum had the crawling feeling in his gut that the chase wasn't over.

He hadn't seen a single bullet hit the body and make it jerk. Even worse, he hadn't *felt* that he'd been on target.

"I'm going down to check it out," he said suddenly.

"What? You will not! There is no time!" protested Rodriguez.

"There's all the time in the world," said Slocum. "When I do a job, it's done right. Count on the same being true when we rob the gold shipments."

"But the Federales . . ." Rodriguez's voice trailed off.

"What Federales?"

"There is a patrol of them not far from the mouth of this canyon. We cannot go down without drawing them like *moscas.*"

"I'll be down and back before you leave." Slocum looked up and judged it to be a little past four in the afternoon. A good time to die, especially if you were an Arizona Ranger. It gave the scavengers plenty of time to find you before the night creatures came out.

"No! You do not go down alone. I will accompany you. I and two others. Those two." Rodriguez pointed out the apprehensive men he wanted to volunteer.

"Suit yourself. I want his scalp."

"You are not like the Yaqui," murmured Rodriguez. "You do not take the scalp. Tell me this."

"I didn't know the Yaquis did that," Slocum admitted.

"They take them and put the scalps on their children's dolls. They use them in religious ceremonies, especially during Pascua."

"During Easter?" This startled Slocum.

"They are very religious, the Yaquis. They were taught by the Jesuits."

"Never heard of a priest taking a scalp," said Slocum, leading his horse down a steep path along the face of the cliff.

"The Yaquis are very imaginative. They consider it part of their celebration, along with nailing one of their own onto a cross. They torture their victims to get the scalps, too."

Slocum heard genuine dread in Rodriguez's voice. That he spoke this way about the Yaquis in front of two of his men told Slocum that the fear was deep-rooted.

He was more afraid of the poor path and the treacherous footing. More than once his horse slipped, making Slocum wish he had come down by himself, leaving the paint at the top of the cliff. As the trail wound away and back, Slocum lost sight of the Ranger's body. It didn't matter much. Within ten minutes they were on the floor of the canyon near the pond formed by one of the two waterfalls.

Slocum slipped the thong off his Colt Navy's hammer. He wanted to be ready for anything.

And he was—except for what he found.

"*Ojalá qué sí,*" exclaimed Rodriguez. "Where did he go? He must be smoke."

"Or a ghost," complained the *pistolero* just behind Slocum. "He turned into vapor and left to haunt the canyon. This is an unclean place. I do not want to stay."

"Damnit!" flared Slocum. "He's not a ghost. He's just a man. And he's not dead. The son of a bitch got away again. I'm going to track him down."

Slocum dropped to the ground and studied the scuffs in the thin, rocky dirt. He found where Johnson had lain, playing possum. When they had vanished around the outjutting of rock, the Ranger had rushed to his horse and ridden like the wind. He had seen he was trapped in a box canyon; he had retreated along the stream toward the mouth of the canyon at the first chance.

"We've got to stop him," Slocum said. "He can't have more than a ten-minute head start on us."

"But no," complained Rodriguez. "We dare not follow. The Federales will find us if we chase him. They are on patrol not two miles from this very spot."

"I don't give a good goddamn if the entire Mexican

Army led by Porfirio Díaz himself is out there. *I want Buck Johnson!*"

Slocum heard Rodriguez protest again as he swung into the saddle and started after the elusive Ranger. Rapid Spanish complaints were exchanged between Rodriguez and his men. Slocum didn't care what they did or didn't do. He wanted Buck Johnson.

"You lead us all into danger, Slocum," said Rodriguez. The bandit leader rode beside him while the other two *pistoleros* trotted along the far side of the stream.

"He can't get up the cliffs. We'd see him." Slocum focused solely on tracking. The hoofprints in the soft mud were as plain a trail as he'd ever followed. The Ranger had had no chance to cover his trail—and no need. There was only one way out of the canyon, and they all knew it.

"There, ahead," said Slocum. "He's not got that much of a lead on us after all." He saw the occasional flash of a man's outline through the dense vegetation. For someone just off the hot Sonoran Desert, this canyon was an oasis. For Slocum intent on finding his quarry, it was a jungle.

"Let us hurry, then," said Rodriguez. The man's nervousness grew the closer they got to the mouth of the canyon.

"There ahead!" Slocum pulled his rifle out and started to squeeze off the killing shot. The Winchester's hammer fell on flesh. Rodriguez let out a small moan, but the sharp recoil and loud report from a firing rifle never came.

Slocum jerked the rifle, and Rodriguez's hand followed. "What the hell are you doing?"

Rodriguez had reached over and shoved the fleshy web stretching from his thumb to his index finger between hammer and firing pin, preventing a discharge.

"You doom us all to perdition if you fire, Señor Slocum," Rodriguez said. "Look."

Rodriguez pulled his hand back and sucked at the tiny well of blood fountaining from his minor wound. Slocum looked past the *pistolero* leader and saw the column of Federales. More than fifty soldiers rode down a canyon leading away at right angles to the box canyon where they watched.

If Slocum had fired, the soldiers would have come to find the cause of the fuss. And Slocum, Rodriguez, and the others would have been forced back into the trap where they had tried to catch Buck Johnson.

Fifty armed Federales against the four of them would have been as much a mismatch as the dozen against Johnson.

But there was one difference. Buck Johnson had escaped, and they wouldn't be that lucky.

6

"We are doomed!" moaned Jaime Rodriguez as they rode deeper into the box canyon. "The Federales have seen us and are onto our trail even as I speak!"

"Shut up and listen carefully," snapped Slocum. He was still angry over losing Buck Johnson. The Arizona Ranger had been within his grasp, and he had allowed him to escape. Although the Ranger couldn't know who had laid this ambush for him, Slocum wanted to put the matter to rest—in a grave.

"What do you have to say to me, gringo?" Rodriguez turned and sneered. The gold tooth had lost some of its luster as it poked past the *pistolero*'s curled lip.

"No advice, I just want you to *listen*. Do you hear hooves?"

"Aiee—no," admitted Rodriguez. "They might sneak up upon us, though. The Federales are very crafty."

"Why bother? They outnumber us. If they knew we were even here, they'd be on us, like *moscas*, as you said."

"Yes, like flies to shit," agreed Rodriguez. The bandit

leader brightened. "If they do not chase us, we can get back up the side of the canyon and to safety. From the rim we will vanish. They will never be able to find us!"

"Let's get up to the canyon rim before we start gloating," muttered Slocum. Even though the company of Federales hadn't seen them—and he had Rodriguez's quick thinking in stopping his shot at the fleeing Johnson to thank for that—they might turn into the canyon just to scout it out. Slocum knew it would take a minimum of an hour to climb back up out of the canyon. Both hindering them and aiding them in their desire to remain hidden from the Federales was the sun going down. In the steep-walled canyons, it was already turning to dusk.

Three hours after their ill-fated attempt to bushwhack the Arizona Ranger, they gained the canyon's edge. Darkness had fallen, turning the trail into a treacherous path. Slocum was never happier to see the cheery glow of the *pistoleros'* campfires when they rounded a sharp turn in the path.

He quickly changed his mind. He could be happier. Consuela stood to one side, eyes only for him.

"A celebration!" called Rodriguez, making his stallion prance. "We have defeated the Federales!"

A loud cheer went up. Slocum looked at the two men who had accompanied them to the canyon floor. They shrugged, then joined in. They were swamped by others demanding to be told of their heroic exploits. Slocum knew that before the night ended those two would become the bravest revolutionaries in all Mexico.

He led his horse to the corral and tended the faithful paint. The horse seemed to appreciate the chance to rest and eat. He patted the horse's neck and then left. Even though there wouldn't be guards on the corral tonight because of the celebration, he thought horse thievery was unlikely.

Slocum looked out into the darkness of the Bacatete Mountains and wondered about how infrequent horse theft was here. He knew Rodriguez's fear of the Yaqui Indians was real. They might not be the barbarians the *pistolero* made them out to be, but Slocum figured they wouldn't be adverse to sneaking into a Mexican camp and stealing a few horses. Rodriguez's band, after all, had camped in their mountains.

"There will be no horses taken this night," came a soft voice.

"You know Rodriguez's little secret, don't you?" he asked Consuela. "You know there's nothing to celebrate."

"Victories are small and far apart. Let them enjoy themselves." She came out of the shadows and stood beside him.

Slocum hadn't noticed how tall she was before. The top of her head came to his nose, and he was over six feet tall. Consuela had changed from her ragged dress into one in little better repair. In spite of this, he thought she looked like a princess.

Bearing had much to do with it. Consuela never walked hunched over. She had a fierce pride that radiated like the noonday sun. Head held high, she seemed indomitable. And she was very, very pretty.

"You like my hair in this style?" she asked coyly.

Slocum hadn't noticed her long, straight black hair done up in a pony tail. He had been too intent staring into the dark pools of her eyes. He could lose himself in them and never care.

"There'll be a full moon tonight," he said.

"Oh?" She batted her long eyelashes at him and half turned. "Do you turn into a . . . wolf?"

Slocum pulled away slightly. He had been thinking how nice it would be to celebrate Rodriguez's "victory" with Consuela. That would cause nothing but trouble. He still hadn't decided what Consuela's position was in the camp. He knew she slept with Rodriguez. The *pistolero* made that obvious at every turn.

But Slocum couldn't see Consuela as belonging to Rodriguez, not in the sense that he owned her. She was too independent for that. That raised new questions in his mind. She didn't love the revolutionary. At times she sounded as if she admired him for what he attempted, but love? Slocum didn't read that in the cards.

"You hesitate," she said softly. "There is no need. Jaime will be with his men most of the night. There is ample tequila and pulque to amuse them until the dawn."

"He might come looking for you."

She shrugged. With a haughty toss of her head that made the long black pony tail snap, she said, "Let him look. I am not his property."

"What are you?" he asked bluntly.

"I am not a *puta*," she said, anger rising. "I do not chase after Jaime's camp to fuck his men."

"Didn't reckon you were doing that," Slocum said. "Can't rightly figure what you *are* doing with him, though. Are you a prisoner? At times it looks that way."

"He kidnapped me from my papa's hacienda," Consuela said. "I am the youngest daughter of a wealthy *patrón*, Don Diego de la Madrid."

Slocum stared at her in amazement. Even north of the border everyone had heard of Don Diego. The de la Madrid family owned thousands of acres of land along the Arizona–New Mexico Territory border. Slocum wondered why there weren't more Federales patrolling the area. Don Diego could command thousands of troops to search for his errant daughter, if he chose to do so.

Consuela de la Madrid spun and walked off into the shadows, her skirt rustling softly. Slocum followed the sound of the skirt and her bare legs moving against it.

"Consuela?" he called.

Slocum found himself pressed back against a stony wall, his arms filled with passionate woman. Consuela's lips sought his. He didn't fight her off. She pressed her lush body against him hard. The kiss was even harder.

She broke off and said, "You are not like Jaime. You are different. I can tell."

"He kidnapped you from your father's hacienda? Yet you seem to stay here of your own accord. You even said you slept with him."

"I fuck him, I do not love him. Why do I do this?" She pushed away and almost faded into the shadows once more. "I protect myself. If Jaime claims me for his own, the others leave me alone. Where can I go? I am at their mercy."

"You could have escaped. The Federales must be looking for you. Get word to them, and they'll return you to Don Diego."

"Why do you think I desire to return to my home? My papa treated me badly. He beat me. Jaime does not do that."

"You said he's—"

"So did my papa," Consuela said, her anger burning hotly in the warm night. "You do not know him. He is an animal. To the peons, he is a saint among men. To his family, he is a devil!"

"What of your mother?"

"She pretends not to know. My sisters are all married and away from this. Papa turned down suitor after suitor because he wanted me for himself. Do you not see why I chose to go with Jaime when he rode by?"

"You weren't kidnapped as much as you wanted to go with him, is that it?"

"A little of each," she admitted. "I was young and desirable. Jaime had been in these accursed mountains for too long. He had not seen any woman, other than the Yaqui women, for many weeks."

Slocum said nothing. Consuela de la Madrid was a victim as surely as any he'd heard of. She had been used to the wealth and position afforded by the de la Madrid name, yet she had endured incest and beatings at her father's hand. Escape had been unthinkable in her society, and she had no one to turn to.

Jaime Rodriguez must have looked like a true savior on his white stallion and with his arrogant ways.

"Do not pity me, John Slocum," she said. "I do not want that."

"What do you want?" he asked. He reached out and caught her arm. He pulled her close again.

"I want you!"

Their kiss deepened until Slocum was left gasping for breath. He knew how foolish this was. The *pistolero* leader considered this woman his personal property. If he caught them together, Slocum knew torture would only be the beginning. He might linger for days before dying. And what Rodriguez might do to Consuela was beyond reckoning.

He knew this—and he couldn't push her away.

His hands moved down her sides, around her trim waist, and held her close. Then he began exploring her lush body, touching bare skin through the tears in her blouse, finding a hardness at the crest of each breast that told him she wanted him as much as he did her.

"There, oh, yes, John, there. Touch me there!" She shoved her chest forward so that her breasts crushed into the palms of his hands.

He tweaked her nipples through the soft cotton. Consuela gasped and threw her head back, exposing her neck. He kissed her lightly on the throat. She moaned and began moving against him in a way he knew he could never resist.

Common sense fled. He had to possess her. Now. Here. To hell with Rodriguez and his banditos.

He kissed Consuela hard on the lips even as he cupped her breasts and lifted. She came up onto her toes. She threw her arms around his neck and hung on to him.

"Not here," she gasped. "It is too close to the camp. We must go farther away where we cannot be heard."

"Where?"

She took his hand and pulled him into the night. Slocum followed, aware that she was right. Consuela de la Madrid was gorgeous and he wanted her, but was his lust going to end in death? Rodriguez was the jealous type. Slocum knew that from the way the *pistolero* put his arm around Consuela's shoulders, kissed her in public, and paraded her around for his men to see.

To him she was only a token of his power.

As they struggled along the rocky, winding trail that led to a sentry post, Slocum's hand went to his six-shooter.

Consuela gripped his wrist and said quietly, "There is no one here tonight. They are in camp celebrating the great victory over the Federales."

"Some victory," scoffed Slocum. "We weren't caught. *That's* the victory."

"You did not even find the Ranger?"

Slocum heaved a deep sigh. He didn't want to talk about that. He wanted to forget Buck Johnson and the threat he still posed. What he craved was close, her musky woman scent arousing him more than ever before.

He pulled Consuela into the circle of his arms and stared into her dark eyes. "I've found you. That's even better," he said.

Again they kissed. The woman's tongue slipped from between her full lips and caressed his, dueling erotically and arousing him even more.

He stripped away her blouse and exposed the full mounds of her dark, warm breasts. He bent over and tongued his way between those succulent mounds. Consuela squealed in pleasure.

"More, John, it feels so good. More!"

He licked his way up one slope and toyed with the hard button he found there, then slid down into the valley of flesh once more and spiraled upward on the other breast. The woman turned slightly. The light from the rising full moon came over Slocum's shoulder and shone directly on the area that he was working on so aggressively. Wherever his tongue touched it left a streak of shining silver on her flesh.

Slocum sucked hard and caught her left nipple between lips and teeth. He gnawed gently. As he did, Consuela's legs gave way. She sank toward the rocky ground.

"I cannot bear this," she gasped out. "You do things to me no man has ever done before."

Slocum saw that making love on the sharp-edged rock of the sentry post wasn't going to do either of their hides any good.

"We can't lie here. We'll have to make—"

"Oh, John, we can't stop now!"

She came to her knees and began fumbling at his belt. He helped, casting aside his cross-draw holster with the Colt in it. By this time, Consuela had shucked his trousers down around his knees and was fumbling inside his long johns.

"What is this? A friend has come to see me!" She touched the tip of his erection with her tongue. It was Slocum's turn to go weak in the knees. She did things with her tongue to his manhood that he hadn't thought were possible.

He looked down and saw himself vanishing into her mouth. When he pulled away from her ruby lips, he saw her spit glistening in the moonlight just as his had done. He had turned from flesh and blood into the purest silver.

Her hands cupped his balls and bounced them tenderly. He groaned and took an involuntary step away. Weakness washed over him like a warm summer rain. Slocum reached out and found a large rock behind him. He braced himself against it as Consuela slithered up him like a snake climbing a tree.

"This will do," she said softly. "It must! I need you.

I need to feel *this* inside me!" She clutched at his throbbing erection and tugged it toward her.

Slocum's hands slid down the sides of her sleek young body once more, this time gathering her skirts into bunches. He lifted, exposing her long legs and nut-brown thighs. He kept raising her skirts until he found the furred triangle nestled between those wondrous thighs.

She parted her legs and scooted forward. Slocum felt himself touching the dampness of her nether lips, then sliding easily into the woman's heated interior. They both gasped as she surrounded him, as he impaled her.

Slocum leaned back, his head resting on the cool rock. He stared up at the rising full moon. The bright argent disk swam in front of his eyes. For a moment he thought he was going blind, then realized thin ice clouds obscured the moon. Never had he felt this excited, this sure of himself.

Rodriguez didn't matter. His heavily-armed revolutionary band didn't matter. The threat of the Arizona Ranger and the Federales and the Yaquis didn't matter. Nothing mattered. All he needed was in the circle of his arms, pressing closely against his belly, holding herself firmly onto his cock.

"Move, John. Move! I need to feel you burning me up inside."

"If I do, I may not be able to last very long," he told her honestly.

"It has been a long time since you had a woman?" she teased. She kissed lightly at his chin and ears.

"I've *never* had a woman like you," he said. His strong arms circled her waist and lifted her off her feet.

Slocum swung around and stood with his feet spread wide. She hung suspended at his waist, his fleshy shaft hidden away inside her clinging, moist interior. He began bouncing her up and down, slowly at first and then faster as their passions mounted.

His balls tightened. His cock strained. It felt as if his loins had been filled with molten lead. Slocum couldn't get enough of Consuela. He kissed her lips and eyes and bit at her neck.

For her part, Consuela tensed and relaxed around his buried pillar. She let him support her at the waist and threw her arms and head back, her long black hair touching the rocky ground. Her strong thighs locked firmly around his waist, she began undulating.

Slocum kept bouncing her up and down even as Consuela began the slow, circular grinding that threatened to rob him of his control. The heat along his length grew. And the volcano in his balls churned and seethed.

"Can't hold back," he moaned through clenched teeth. He looked across her body and saw her perfect breasts in the moonlight.

Slocum erupted.

The rush of his seed into her sensitive channel triggered Consuela's passions. She came hard, her legs almost crushing Slocum as she sobbed and wailed in the tumultuous release of desire.

Her legs went limp suddenly. Slocum struggled to keep her from falling to the ground. Consuela got her legs under her and stared up at him, her eyes aglow.

"You are marvelous," she whispered. "Never has a man made me feel so alive!"

He lifted her and kissed her hard. He felt himself stirring again. He wanted more from her—and he knew she wanted it from him.

Slocum jerked up, his head turning when he heard footsteps on the path to this sentry post.

"Someone's coming," he said. He pushed Consuela away and pulled up his drawers. He grabbed his gunbelt and slid the Colt from its holster. He didn't want to kill anyone, but he would if it meant Rodriguez finding out what had just happened.

The bandito wasn't likely to be the forgiving or sharing kind.

Consuela hurriedly pulled her skirt down and straightened her blouse. "There, over there," she said urgently. A small rock afforded a measure of protection. They dropped behind it just as a *pistolero* staggered to the summit. He walked on shaky legs to the far side of the post and settled against a rock.

"He is *borracho*," whispered Consuela. "Wait a moment. Wait and we can slip past him."

Slocum saw that she was right. The sentry pulled out a bottle. From the odor carried on the light night breeze, it was the potent tequila the Mexicans preferred to decent Kentucky whiskey. The guard knocked back several strong belts, then belched loudly. The next sound Slocum heard was loud snoring.

Consuela took his hand and led him back down the path into the camp. The sentry had never known they were there.

When Slocum saw Rodriguez and the wild expression on his face from too much alcohol, he knew the bandit's leader hadn't missed them.

That took some of the immediate threat away, but when Slocum looked at Consuela, he knew there would be other times. Would he continue to be so lucky? Or would Jaime Rodriguez eventually figure out someone else was bedding his woman?

7

Jaime Rodriguez looked from Slocum to Consuela de la Madrid and back. He frowned so hard that wrinkles corrugated his forehead. Slocum began to worry that the *pistolero* had somehow learned of their assignation the night of the celebration.

Slocum kept a poker face. To give any hint of nervousness would be dangerous. Rodriguez was like a wild animal at times. Show any small weakness and he went straight for the throat.

"You are ill, Consuela?" the bandito asked. "Go and lie down. Rest. Save your strength for me later. You do not need to disturb us until after we have finished with our plans."

"What do I care for your foolish robbery plans?" she said haughtily, tossing her head and sending her long black hair streaming like an arrogant banner in the hot wind. She gave Slocum a lingering look, bent and kissed Rodriguez quickly, and walked off.

"She is a fine woman, no?" said Rodriguez, staring at the departing woman. "Many men would steal and kill for a woman like her. I would." His dark eyes fixed on Slocum's cold green ones, as if challenging him to disagree.

"I can see that," Slocum said noncommittally. He turned back to the map of the Bacatete Mountains the *pistolero* had spread on the ground. Four rocks held the corners down against the soft wind that had caught Consuela's hair. Slocum forced such thoughts from his mind. He had to concentrate completely on planning the train robbery, not Rodriguez's woman.

Slocum found that increasingly difficult. Consuela de la Madrid occupied much of his waking thoughts.

"You think this is a good plan?" asked the bandit leader, forcing Slocum back to the matter at hand.

"I need more information. I assume you will know if there'll be gold on any given shipment."

"But of course. Why guard empty cars? The railroad tracks moan under the weight of so many Federales watching the gold."

Slocum shook his head. "They might be luring you into a trap. Lots of soldiers, no gold." He also considered the other possibility. The government might send a shipment completely unguarded, thinking rightly that Rodriguez would attack only the trains laden with soldiers.

This seemed less likely. From all Rodriguez had told him, the Yaquis were as likely to hijack the train as the revolutionaries.

"In this pass, the train slows. Is it not a good place to attack?" demanded Rodriguez.

"I'd have to see it for myself. It might be." Slocum felt the iron jaws of a trap closing around him. Rodriguez was insistent on this pass, and Slocum couldn't decide why. There must be any of a hundred places where the narrow-gauge railroad engine had to struggle up a steep grade. Slocum wasn't even sure those were the best places to attack. A few boulders pushed across the tracks might serve the same purpose and give them a better escape route across easier terrain.

"I can ride down the tracks in front of the train," Rodriguez said. "They will see me and know true fear."

"Why not just wait till the train comes to a complete stop, then show yourself? Why warn the soldiers?"

"I am a hero to my people. I must act like one."

Slocum said nothing. Rodriguez wanted the glory but didn't want to risk his neck getting it.

"Dead heroes are a nickel a peck. Rich revolutionaries are a scarcer breed."

"What do you say? That I should not take part in this robbery to aid our glorious revolution?"

"That might not be a bad idea. Your men know who their leader is. Everyone in these mountains knows who the *jefe* is," Slocum said, feeding the man's ego. If he could keep Rodriguez occupied—with a small band of *pistoleros* as bodyguards—he stood a good chance of slipping away and heading back north.

The *pistolero* had done all he could to stop Buck Johnson. Slocum felt the growing need to return to Arizona and find out for himself if the Ranger had made it back alive. Even more to the point, he wanted free of Rodriguez and his would-be revolutionary bandits. Their fight wasn't his. Staying could only complicate his life.

Besides that, he had three men to look up. Delling, Ballard, and Ogelvie had money that belonged to him. It might not be much, but he had risked his neck for it and was going to get his fair share. And one of them might have put Buck Johnson on his trail. Slocum hadn't forgotten the unexpected meeting in Hermosilla. He had two new scars from the Arizona Ranger's bullets to show for that encounter.

Getting Rodriguez out of the way during the train robbery went a long way toward getting free, he knew. The revolutionary leader would be more interested in gold than in chasing down Slocum.

"A drink, Señor Slocum?" came a soft voice. Startled, he looked up. Consuela's shadow fell across the map.

"Thanks," he said, taking the battered tin cup of water from her. The woman's fingers slipped across his, lingering for a split second longer than a casual touch. Slocum's heart raced. Leaving Consuela might be harder than he thought. She wasn't here of her own accord, and she certainly didn't want to return to Don Diego's hacienda.

Slocum tried to work out a plan where Consuela could accompany him after he got away from Rodriguez. Nothing fell together for him. He'd have to leave her behind, as much as he hated the notion.

"You are ill, Slocum?" asked Rodriguez.

"No, why?"

"You got this faraway look, as if someone walked on your grave. If you do not feel good, go rest. This plan will take a while to develop. The train is not due for another two days."

"I'm fine," Slocum insisted. He wanted to hit Consuela. The woman openly laughed. She knew what thoughts raced through his mind, and she loved the confusion she caused.

"There must be a strange illness afflicting my camp," mused Rodriguez. "You and Consuela are both pining away, eh?" Again Rodriguez cast a sharp eye at Slocum.

"I want to go to the site now. We might need the extra time to set up for the robbery. It's not going to work right if we simply ride up and try to hijack the gold shipment."

"Like the actor, we should rehearse, is that what you are saying? This is a difficult thing to do. My men grow restless and do not always wait as they should for the proper moment."

Slocum saw that Rodriguez had trouble maintaining order in the camp. Since the revelry two nights earlier, most of the men had stayed drunk on the potent tequila.

"It'd be a good chance to get them back into fighting

trim," suggested Slocum. "Once out on the trail it's harder to keep drinking like this and stay in the saddle."

Rodriguez laughed heartily. "You are not Mexican. We can drink and ride for weeks without end!" He sobered and tapped the gold tooth with his right index finger. Slocum wondered again how the bandito had lost the little finger on his right hand. Every gesture Rodriguez made accentuated the loss, as if showing the world what a brave vaquero he was.

"Still," said Rodriguez, thinking hard, "you might have something. I tell them we ride against the Federales, *then* rob the train. That sounds good." He clapped Slocum on the shoulder. "I knew you were an excellent tactician. You have the look about you." Jaime Rodriguez shot to his feet and began roaring orders, getting his men to their horses and ready for travel.

Slocum looked up at Consuela. She smiled wickedly and said in a low voice, "That is not all you are good at." She spun so that her skirt flared away from her fine legs and rolled her hips to give Slocum a hint of what he was missing.

Slocum was as glad to be away from the danger posed by Consuela as he was to get on the trail. Leaving her behind would be hard, but he had another plan. Getting away from Rodriguez and his men was at the top of the list.

Then he had a score to settle with Buck Johnson.

"We have provisions for a week," said Rodriguez. "That will be enough, no?"

Slocum nodded. He didn't care if they had enough along for ten years. As soon as they stopped the train and began shooting it up, he would fade into the shadows. Living off the land in the Sonora Desert wasn't easy, but he had done it on his way to Hermosilla. He could do it on his way back to Nogales.

"You stare into space again. Do you plan the robbery even more carefully?"

"Something like that," Slocum said. "I wouldn't want anything to go wrong."

"No, we wouldn't," Rodriguez said, a hint of menace in his voice. "After all our efforts on your behalf to stop the Arizona Ranger, you owe us much."

Slocum rode out of the camp, trying not to look at Consuela. He found it impossible. From the corner of his eye, he saw her waving—and he knew it wasn't Rodriguez she was waving good-bye to. It was for the best, he kept telling himself, that he wouldn't return to Rodriguez's camp. Playing with Consuela was worse than playing with fire. Getting burned was preferable to dying.

"We will approach the pass where we rob the train from the desert floor," said Rodriguez. "We will ride along the railroad tracks and then back into the mountains."

Something about the forceful way he said it convinced Slocum the *pistolero* was talking to bolster his own courage.

"Why not just go directly there, then backtrack until we find a good spot to hit the train?" Slocum asked.

"The Yaquis," Rodriguez admitted reluctantly, "have been active in the area. We do not want to antagonize them before we attack the gold shipment."

Slocum digested this as they rode. Rodriguez was scared shitless of the *indios*. For all his posturing and chest beating, he wasn't much of a leader. The only way he'd stayed in power was sheer luck, from all Slocum could see. Any leader worth his salt should have been able to plan the gold-train robbery.

When Slocum came to that thought, he stopped. Rodriguez wasn't *too* stupid. He really didn't need Slocum to do any planning for him, in spite of everything he'd said. Slocum began to think that Rodriguez was going to use him in some way the bandito hadn't revealed.

Whatever was brewing in Rodriguez's brain, it wasn't likely to bode well for him, Slocum knew.

They rode the trails along the western slopes of the Bacatete Mountains until nearly dusk. Rodriguez lifted his hand and brought the column of men to a halt when he saw an approaching horsemen.

"One of your scouts?" asked Slocum.

"*Sí*, that is Jorge. He has eyes everywhere, or so it seems. Nothing escapes him." Rodriguez's mood had lightened considerably since they had been on the trail. Slocum's suggestion that this jaunt might sober up the men had proven accurate. Although some grumbled, none was able to drink and keep up the pace and maneuver along the rocky, treacherously narrow mountain paths.

"*Jefe*," cried the scout, reining in just in front of Rodriguez. "There is a band of them."

"Yaquis?"

"No, no, Federales! At least twenty of them. They camp for the night nearby. You would have stumbled into their camp had you kept riding."

"They block the path we take to get to the railroad," muttered Rodriguez. "What can we do?" He smiled broadly, as if the answer had just come to him. "We will kill them in their sleep!"

"They are alert, *Jefe*."

"What makes them this way, Jorge?" Rodriguez asked suspiciously. "Is it—"

"Yaqui war parties are everywhere," Jorge affirmed breathlessly. "The Federales try to fight them at every turn. They fail. *Los indios* take no prisoners. The Federales started with more than thirty."

Slocum listened silently. The Yaquis had killed fully a third of the Federale company. He didn't need Jorge to tell him there hadn't been many, if any, losses on the Yaquis' part.

"We can finish the work the Yaquis started," said

Rodriguez. "Prepare for a fight!" he called over his shoulder to his ragtag troops. "We will whet their appetite for fighting, then pick off the gold shipment like a freshly bloomed rose!"

"Isn't there any way around the Federales?" Slocum asked. He didn't want to risk a fight with them for no reason.

"None," said Jorge. "They camp across this road. If you go to the railroad, you must pass them."

"You might take too many casualties to rob the train," Slocum pointed out. "Is it worth jeopardizing your chance at the gold to tangle with the Federales?"

"It is always that way. Only by killing them all can we be sure of our victory!"

"Let Jorge and me scout the camp," he said. "I'll report back if there's a way to avoid them."

"We do not avoid the Federales. We kill them! Men, prepare for combat!"

Slocum blinked in surprise when Rodriguez lifted his rifle in the air, fired, and got his men racing along the rocky road behind him. Jorge looked at Slocum and shrugged, as if saying, "He is crazy, but he is my *jefe*." Jorge swung in behind, joining in the cries as Rodriguez's small war party attacked blindly.

Slocum considered hanging back and waiting to see the result of the battle. If the Federales won, Slocum was free to do as he pleased. He could ride off and not worry about Rodriguez and his plans for holding up the train. But if Rodriguez happened to be victorious, Slocum knew the *pistolero* would track him to the ends of the earth to avenge perceived cowardice.

Slocum trotted along behind the last of the revolutionaries, warily listening for their reception in the Federales' camp. The sudden volley told him the soldiers had laid a trap and cut down the leading elements of Rodriguez's charge.

As Slocum rounded a bend in the road, he saw the

scout, Jorge, heading down a side canyon, putting his fancy Spanish silver spurs to his horse's flanks. Slocum made a split-second decision. He went after the fleeing scout. It took more than ten minutes of hard riding before he overtook the man.

Jorge looked back to see who was pursuing him. His dark eyes showed white all around. Fear was etched on his face.

"Stop!" shouted Slocum. When the fleeing man began whipping his horse with his reins, Slocum knew it was more than fear pushing Jorge. Guilt drove him, too.

The canyon floor turned flat and gave Slocum his chance. His paint strove to keep even with the other man's horse. Slocum leaned over and reached out, his fingers finding the flapping edge of Jorge's bandanna. Slocum caught it and tugged. Jorge flew backward off his horse, landing hard on the rocks beside the road.

Slocum used his knees to control his horse as he fought to keep his own balance. He swung around and returned to where the frightened man was picking himself up off the ground. His right arm dangled at a crazy angle. He had broken it in the fall.

"Do not kill me, señor," pleaded the fallen man. "I did it only because they promised not to harm my family. I have a wife and three small children. The Federales are very cruel. You cannot know. They are animals. Worse!"

Slocum drew his Colt Navy and aimed it at Jorge's head. "If you don't start walking, I'll have to bury you right here. I don't want to do that."

"*Gracias*," Jorge babbled.

"I don't want to do that because the ground is too hard. I'd have to leave you for the buzzards."

Jorge blanched and backed away from Slocum. The muzzle of Slocum's gun moved slightly to indicate where he wanted the man to walk. Jorge took off at a steady clip, looking back over his shoulder often to be sure that Slocum had decided not to shoot him in the back.

Twenty minutes later, they got to the Federales camp. Slocum approached cautiously. He didn't know if Rodriguez had bulled his way through to victory or if the Federales had been successful in their ambush.

The loud crowing and boisterous laughter told him Jaime Rodriguez had carried the day.

Silence fell over the camp as Slocum rode in with his captive.

"I had wondered what became of you, Slocum," said the bandit leader. "We rode into an ambush."

"How'd you get out of it?" asked Slocum, curious. He did a quick count and saw that Rodriguez couldn't have lost more than two men. Three had minor wounds that had already been bandaged. For such a skirmish, this was incredibly good luck.

"We decoyed them into revealing themselves. I thought there might be . . . trouble," he said slowly, drawing the words out. "We came up on their flank. They did not expect this tactic. They fell quickly to our guns."

"Why'd you suspect a trap?"

"A traitor in our ranks, one who rode at the end of the column," Rodriguez said, his eyes hard on Slocum.

"How would you punish such a traitor?" Slocum asked, his fingers tightening around the butt of his pistol.

"In the only way possible!"

A dozen shots rang out from the men in a half circle behind Rodriguez. Slocum sat up straighter in the saddle, then realized the bullets hadn't found a home in his body. Jorge twitched and jerked on the ground at his feet.

"Thank you for bringing the traitor back to us for justice," said Rodriguez. He gave Slocum a meaningful look, then spun and stalked off.

Slocum got the message. Jaime Rodriguez did not tolerate spies in his band.

He wondered what Rodriguez would think of someone bedding his woman and planning to turn tail and run at the first chance? Slocum decided he already knew the answer to that.

8

"Traitors are everywhere," opined Jaime Rodriguez. "I find them all over. Most of my men are good, loyal, brave. A few are like Jorge. They sell out at the slightest flash of gold under their noses." Rodriguez looked at Slocum out of the corner of his eye. "Did he confess to you how much the Federales offered him?"

"He said they threatened his wife and three children."

"A coward, then, and a fool. He could have gotten hundreds of pesos in gold from them for betraying me." Rodriguez puffed himself up and sat even taller on the white stallion. "There is a reward of five hundred pesos on my head."

"I don't doubt it," said Slocum. He was still uneasy over how the *pistoleros* had shot down Jorge. The man had deserved it, but Slocum had to wonder if they'd think he was a traitor too when he finally lit out for the border. Slocum wasn't going to betray Rodriguez and the others, but he wasn't playing square with them either.

"It will soon be double that. Ten times!" Rodriguez took it as a matter of honor how much reward money rested on his head. He never thought that, when the amount of money grew big enough, he'd have to look over his shoulder at his own men. Which of the so-called revolutionaries wouldn't turn Jaime Rodriguez in for five thousand pesos? Slocum knew they'd be lined up waiting to do it—and assume command of the banditos after back-shooting their leader.

"How are you going to carry the gold after we get it off the train?" Slocum asked, changing the subject. He didn't want to hear any more of Rodriguez's high-flown bragging. The *pistolero* was getting calluses on his hand from patting himself on the back.

"We have ways," Rodriguez said mysteriously.

Seeing that Slocum wasn't buying it, Rodriguez rode closer and said in a low voice, "There will be casualties when we take the train, no?"

Slocum allowed as to how that was likely.

"We will use the horses lacking riders. They are strong animals. Each should be able to carry an amount of gold equal to its present rider."

"How many horses do you reckon will be freed up this way?" asked Slocum.

"Four, perhaps five."

"You're going to settle for only six hundred pounds of gold? How small are these shipments?" Slocum wanted to goad Rodriguez. He was irritated by the man's arrogance.

"This is a great deal of gold. Your *norteamericano* shipments are larger?"

"Usually it's not worth going after unless it's a ton or more," Slocum lied. He had robbed banks and stage-coaches for less than fifty dollars. At the time he'd done it, the few miserable coins he'd gotten had seemed a fortune.

"We should go north of the border to rob the trains," murmured Rodriguez. He brightened. "But what can we expect in Mexico? The railroad is only narrow-gauge. It cannot carry more than this over the Bacatete Mountain passes."

Slocum didn't reply. They rode through the day and came to a gorge so deep his vision was cut off by purple distance-haze.

"It is *muy bonita*, eh? This is where we will attack the train. The guards can do nothing to stop us."

"No, they can't," agreed Slocum. "And there's not a hell of a lot you can do if they have more firepower. It'd be a . . ." His voice trailed off. Rodriguez didn't look the type to appreciate hearing about Mexican standoffs.

"We can starve them out of their treasure car, if we need to," declared Rodriguez.

"Better to get the gold in a clean attack," said Slocum. His keen eyes worked over the railroad tracks clinging so precariously to the side of the canyon. He wondered how they'd ever built the tracks. The Bacatete Mountains had their share of high passes, but this one was enough to make even the most experienced mountain man dizzy. Strata showed down hundreds of feet on the sheer canyon walls. Slocum thought he heard the pounding of fast-moving water below, possibly the Sonora River or a large tributary.

"Why'd they build like this?" he asked. "Going down to the coast to Guaymas where it's flatter seems a better choice."

"This is a spur running toward the Ocho Pueblos of the Yaquis and then into the heart of Mexico. From the Pacific Coast they bring their gold and ship it to Mexico City. It is our duty to see that the dictators never receive it."

"The Ocho Pueblos?" asked Slocum. He had heard mention of them before but wasn't sure what it meant.

"The Yaquis have eight villages on the banks of the Yaqui River. Cocorit, Bacum, Torim with its wheat fields, Vicam, Potam, Rahun, Huirivis, and Belem were supplied by this railroad until the *indios* revolted. Now the trains go fast past the villages and do not stop."

"Why keep the line open at all?"

A sly look came over Rodriguez's face. "They think to bring in Federales to put down any uprising. They look beyond the current. The Yaquis have been known to talk with dictators. And the greedy bastards in Mexico City want to exploit La Mina Colorada."

"A Yaqui mine?" guessed Slocum.

"Gold. But it is along their river below and in the depths of the Bacatete Mountains where the Yaquis' real wealth is found. Silver. They find silver at every turn in the mountains. It is so rich, nuggets fall from the rock into their waiting hands." The greed and longing in Rodriguez's voice was unmistakable.

"Too bad the Yaquis don't ship their silver out," Slocum said. "Hijacking a shipment or two of such wealth would be enough to keep your revolution going for years."

"We do not antagonize the Yaquis."

"You don't mind robbing the Federales of the gold they guard," Slocum pointed out.

"The Federales do not live in these mountains." Rodriguez shuddered and pointed toward the railroad tracks. "There. Do you not agree that is a good place for the robbery?"

Slocum didn't like the notion of stopping the train when they could reach it only by coming down the tracks from the summit. What he disliked even more was the scant opportunity this afforded him to slip away. He couldn't go past the train, not with his horse. Going uphill meant scaling a cliff—and going down meant a fall of hundreds and hundreds of feet.

In spite of himself, he stared at the long fall past strata of copper and green and red and yellow rock. One mistake would send them plunging to the bottom of the canyon.

"They will not be able to run," said Rodriguez, following Slocum's gaze.

"The Federales or your men?"

Rodriguez blinked, then laughed and slapped Slocum on the back. "I like you, amigo. You have a sense of humor lacking in most of the gringos I have known. It will be a pleasure robbing this train under your guidance."

Slocum knew that Rodriguez had ignored most of the plans they'd laid out back in the *pistolero*'s camp. Whatever the revolutionary was plotting, it didn't bode well for John Slocum.

"You didn't actually *kill* Buck Johnson," Slocum said suddenly.

"So, amigo?"

"So I ought to get a small cut of the gold in payment. Seems fair since you lost him."

Slocum watched Rodriguez and knew he was right in thinking the bandit leader was going to double-cross him. Rodriguez smiled even more broadly and showed the gold tooth. "You are right, Señor Slocum. You will receive an equal share of this gold for your trouble. The Arizona Ranger might still look for you. The gold can be used to get far, far away from him."

The bandit leader motioned for Slocum to precede him. Slocum felt increasingly uneasy having Rodriguez ride behind him. He expected a single bullet to shatter his spine or a knife to drive deep and bloody into his back. Nothing of the sort happened, and they came to the top of the pass, where the railroad construction crews had spent several days preparing a camp.

"This will serve as our base until the train comes at noon tomorrow," said Rodriguez. "Until then, let us rest and prepare. You must instruct the men on their part in the big robbery."

Slocum went over the robbery with a half dozen of the men. Their inattention told him they'd do what they damned well pleased and no gringo was going to order them around. Slocum didn't push the matter. He was getting to the point of wanting to slip off into the night and to hell with what Rodriguez might do. Let the *pistolero* track him down. Slocum wasn't sure he'd give up the gold train in return for the pleasure of killing a lone gringo—but he didn't know.

He didn't even know if there *was* a gold shipment coming. Rodriguez could lie convincingly when the need arose, and Slocum hadn't a clue about what was really in store for him.

Slocum rose quietly and slipped away from his spot near the fire. He went to the crude corral where the horses were penned and tried to soothe his paint. The animal was unusually skittish tonight.

"Whoa, quiet," Slocum said, patting the horse's neck. The animal wasn't having any of it.

Slocum spun, hand on his pistol when he heard rock crunching behind him. Jaime Rodriguez and three of his *pistoleros* stood in a semicircle, rifles leveled. Slocum would have died instantly had he drawn his six-shooter.

"So, Señor Slocum, you do not think to leave us, do you? The night is no place to be roaming alone. The Yaquis are on the prowl. My scouts tell me of their activity up and down the length of the railroad tracks."

"My horse was acting up. I just wanted to quiet it."

"But of course, how silly of me not to realize you always tend your animal in the middle of the night." Rodriguez's sarcasm bit deep. Slocum considered his chances of shooting it out with the four men. The gunmen with Rodriguez weren't as attentive as they might be; they thought their leader was in full command. Slocum was fast enough on the draw to get his Colt Navy out and pump two good shots into Rodriguez. The remaining four could scatter the banditos.

Again, Rodriguez surprised him.

"Or you might have heard our base camp was overrun by Federales."

"What?"

"Do not worry. Word was sent in time. We abandoned much of our supplies, but those can be replaced when we have the gold from this shipment."

"What about those in the camp?"

"Casualties were small. See? Here they come now."

Slocum glanced over his shoulder. A dark line of horses and riders came up the draw. He hadn't heard them because of rags tied over the horses' hooves. Straining, he heard their muffled advance. Slocum gave up all hope of escape this night. Against Rodriguez and his handful of men he stood a chance. Against the entire band he didn't have a snowball's chance in hell of making it.

"John!" came a familiar voice. Slocum stiffened. Consuela de la Madrid was at the head of the column. The woman dropped to the ground when she saw him and ran over.

"It was awful," Consuela cried. "They came from all around. The Federales would have left no one alive! It is a miracle we escaped when we did!"

"Another traitor in our ranks," Rodriguez said solemnly. "We shall deal with him when we discover his identity."

The notion that Rodriguez was going to put him in that role didn't bother Slocum as much as Rodriguez not raising a fuss over Consuela going to him and throwing her arms around his neck. Slocum untangled the woman and pushed her back.

"You can't rob the train with your entire band here," Slocum said. "Escape will be almost impossible."

"Escape will be easier with my army at my back!" Rodriguez laughed. The last Slocum saw of him was the flash of his gold tooth in the faint light coming from the smoldering campfires.

"John, it was terrible!" cried Consuela.

He said nothing to her. He checked his horse one last time, then went back to his bedroll. Consuela sputtered angrily and went to bed down with Rodriguez. Sleep eluded Slocum for hours as he stared into the pitch-black night of the Bacatete Mountains and worried about Jaime Rodriguez. The bandito had not been upset at the notion of losing his base camp to the Federales. If anything, he had seemed happy at the prospect.

Had he turned over the camp in return for a few pesos? Slocum wondered how many games Rodriguez was playing.

Too many was the only answer he could come up with. And the deadly games would continue until they were played out and people died. Slocum didn't want to be one of those who ended up in an unmarked grave, even if that was what Rodriguez intended as his fate.

"We are less than one hour from the train's arrival," said Rodriguez, sitting with his back to the sheer rock and his feet resting on the railroad tracks. "Then we will have real money. You have instructed my men?"

"The ones that bothered to listen," said Slocum. He fumed. He still didn't know how Rodriguez expected to profit by killing him. Unless Consuela had confessed all, the *pistolero* didn't know of their dalliance. Slocum wouldn't put it past the *patrón*'s daughter, though, to do what was in her own best interest. If she thought Rodriguez's ardor for her was waning, she'd sleep with the very devil.

"They listened," Rodriguez said confidently. He sat up and smiled broadly. He rested his hand on the tracks, three fingers pressing into the steel rail. "The train comes. It is early today, a good sign that the gold is aboard."

Slocum had to agree. Keeping to a schedule when you were carrying as much gold as Rodriguez thought was aboard might be dangerous. Better to be ahead of schedule and avoid other bands of late-arriving banditos.

"Amigos!" shouted Rodriguez. "To your places!"

Slocum watched as the *pistoleros* spread out. Rocks on the steep track just beyond a curve would stop the train. The banditos would slide down the sheer cliff from above and land atop the train and take out the Federales guarding the gold. Or so went the plan. Slocum wasn't sure what would happen.

"It is a great distance down, eh?" asked Rodriguez. He put his arm around Slocum's shoulders and forced him to peer down into the canyon. The distance-haze hadn't cleared. If anything, it had thickened and made the bottom of the canyon seem even more distant. Slocum had the image of a man falling forever before being swallowed whole by the mists.

"How did they ever build the railroad?" asked Slocum. "If the Yaquis are as bad as you say, they wouldn't have let crews in here for the months it took to cut a ledge for the tracks."

"The Yaquis benefit from the railroad," Rodriguez said. "When they are not at war with the government, they ship their crops to Guaymas and even to the Pacific Ocean. And always they have their silver. To find those mines would make a man rich beyond avarice." He gave an eloquent shrug. "They do not destroy the tracks because the think they will again be dominant in the region. They are wrong."

Rodriguez's political musings were cut off by the rumble and hiss of the steam engine making its way up the steep slope. Rodriguez waved to his men, then took Slocum by the arm and pulled him back. "Remain beside me. You shall share in my triumph, you who are the architect of it!"

Slocum let an icy calm settle over him. The robbery no longer mattered. He had to get away with his life.

Whatever Rodriguez planned for him would happen quickly—and soon.

The train struggled around the curve in the mountain, then hit the brakes with a loud screech. The steam engine stopped a few feet from the pile of rocks on the tracks. The engineer cursed volubly, thinking this wasn't anything more than a natural rockfall. He yelled for the Federales to get out and clear the track.

Slocum held his breath. He had planned the robbery. He wanted to see how well it worked. A half-dozen uniformed soldiers left the second car and came forward carrying their rifles and long pry bars.

Rodriguez's men opened fire too soon. They cut down the Federales, but they also alerted the ones still in the gold car. The heavy doors slid shut. Slocum heard steel locking bars sliding into place.

"Damnit!" he flared. "They ambushed them too soon. Two men were supposed to get on top of the car and get inside before the others opened fire!"

Rodriguez's face clouded with anger. He whipped around, his rifle leveled at Slocum. His finger tightened, then eased. "Help them. You are the expert. Help them get the gold from the car. It is armored!"

Slocum cursed his own reaction. He should have let Rodriguez hurry off to see to the gold. Now he had the *pistolero* at his back with the rifle.

"You never told me the car had armor plating on it."

Slocum saw now why the train had such difficulty making it up the steep mountain pass. Although it had only five cars, one was lined with steel plate. Short of dynamite, he saw no way to get into the car.

Slocum ducked when a rifle bullet almost took off his hat. He came to rest behind a boulder near the edge of the railroad track. Beside having the car armored, the Federales had cut gun slits in the sides. Those inside could shoot out and be protected from return fire.

"We cannot wait them out," complained Rodriguez,

coming to rest beside Slocum. "There will be another train along within hours, and this one is a troop carrier."

"We'll have Federales coming out our ears then?" asked Slocum.

"Yes!"

Slocum knew starving the guards out of the gold car wasn't likely to work either. They'd have enough supplies inside to outlast any siege.

"Is there steel plating under the car, too?" he asked.

"Yes. It is too thick to cut through."

"Build a fire under it. Roast the Federales inside," said Slocum.

Rodriguez was slow to comprehend, then a grin flowed across his face and the gold tooth came out like the sun from behind a storm cloud. "I knew there was a reason I had you along, Señor Slocum. You are a genius at this train robbing!"

Rodriguez called out instructions. Slocum wished that he had passed along the orders quietly. He didn't want the men inside the gold car to know what was happening until their feet caught on fire. Slocum didn't think they could do anything about a fire being built under them, but he didn't want to take the risk.

"Let me move around—" he started. Rodriguez's rifle muzzle poked into his ribs.

"You stay beside me, Slocum," Rodriguez said. "We will watch our victory unfold together."

Slocum cursed. He had wanted to get to his horse and get the hell away. Rodriguez had blocked his retreat. Slocum looked past the rocks on the track and saw Consuela with two men. They seemed to be guarding her. Slocum cursed to himself. The woman *was* at the center of this. He should never have dallied with her. Laying another man's woman was bad, and when the other man was an arrogant, self-styled revolutionary it was even worse.

"It will not be long now," said Rodriguez. He had lost

four men trying to build the fires. The crackling flames leaped up around the car, seeking the exposed wooden parts. "They fry inside like *indio* bread, eh?" He nudged Slocum in the ribs with his rifle.

Slocum had the feeling that, once the Federales came pouring out and were cut down, he'd die, too.

The explosion stunned him. Bits of shrapnel sailed past his head just as it had during the war. Stunned, Slocum sat on the ground and stared at the remnants of the armored car holding the gold.

"Back, get back!" he heard someone yelling.

The heavy car slipped to its side, propped against the rocky cliff face. As if it had come to rest on ice, the heavy wheels began sliding, taking track and rock with it.

"No!" cried Jaime Rodriguez. "You cannot do this! Do not fall!"

The gold shipment, the car, and the Federales inside slid over the edge of the canyon. The railway car fell slowly through the air, touching the side of the canyon twice before vanishing into the mist below.

9

Slocum watched the gold-laden car disappear into the canyon and continued to stare long after it vanished from sight. It had been a majestic sight in its way, but he couldn't get the sounds out of his head of the Federales inside the falling car screaming. After the second time the railcar crashed into the jagged side of the canyon, the cries had stopped.

"All that gold," he said, more to himself than to Jaime Rodriguez.

"The gold is gone."

Slocum turned at the sound of the choked voice and saw Consuela looking stricken. Her dark eyes searched the canyon for some clue to where the gold had gone.

"You lost the gold, Señor Slocum," said Rodriguez. "Now you will go retrieve it for me."

"What?" Slocum swung on the bandit leader and saw he wasn't joking. The anger on Rodriguez's face brooked no opposition.

"You will get my gold. You will leave now. My scouts say the second train with the two companies of Federales will arrive in less than a half hour. You must be far enough down the canyon side so that they will not follow."

"You're crazy!" Slocum blurted. "I can't get down there. Nobody can. Not even an eagle could—"

"You will go, Señor Slocum. No?" Rodriquez cocked his rifle and pointed it at Slocum's midriff.

Slocum looked from Rodriquez to Consuela and saw the horror written on her face. She wasn't a party to this; she was as shocked as he was by Rodriguez's order.

"Do not worry, señor. You will have company. A half dozen of my best men will accompany you, as will lovely Consuela." Rodriguez grabbed her roughly and shoved her into Slocum's arms. "She seems at home there, eh?"

"You can't make me go down *there*!" Consuela dropped to her knees and pleaded with Rodriguez.

Slocum went cold inside. Consuela's plea meant more than fearing the danger of descent. There was something deadly at the bottom of this gorge—and she knew what it was.

Slocum worked through his options. Fighting Rodriguez with all his men surrounding him was out of the question. Trying to escape back down the tracks gave no good solution to his problems, either. He'd end up running directly into the Federales' guns. Trying to get past Rodriguez and escaping down the other side of the mountain was as likely as fighting his way free.

"Well go," Slocum said.

"You will?" The straightforward answer startled Rodriguez. He had expected him to argue. During the argument, Slocum knew he might have been cut down as an example against failing to obey *el jefe's* every command.

"You're right. It was my fault we lost the gold. I'll fetch it." Slocum knew that the canyon floor offered a better chance of escape than he had on this rocky ledge cut for the railroad. With only a half-dozen men to worry about, he could slip away from them and follow the river at the canyon bottom in whichever direction seemed most likely to get him the hell away from his problems.

He might even be able to take Consuela along. Slocum decided this was the best he could do. And the more he thought on it, the more he knew it was his only hope for staying alive even a few more minutes. He'd learn what she knew and use it, somehow.

"*Bueno*, good, go quickly. Take spare horses for the gold. How many can we give them?" Rodriguez asked a lieutenant. A quick count showed eight horses without riders.

"Jaime, you can't send me down there. Not down *there*!" begged Consuela. "I will do anything. He meant nothing to me. Don't make me go *there*!"

"Ride or fly," he said coldly. "It matters nothing to me which you choose. But you *will* go."

"Come on," Slocum said, grabbing Consuela's arm and pulling her to her feet. "Don't beg. It doesn't do any good." He looked at Rodriguez, wondering anew what the bandito leader's plans had been. When the gold had fallen over the rim of the canyon, those plans had changed. If he was foolish enough to return with the gold, the plans would again come into play.

He just wouldn't return, with or without the gold. Staying alive to escape might prove even more difficult, though.

"No, you don't know what's down there. It is our death to go down this canyon."

"Your horses," said Rodriguez. "*Buena suerte*, my friends. You will need it—and more."

Slocum got a crying Consuela onto a small horse. His own paint shied at the notion of going down the steep path that seemed little more than a foot wide. It started near the railroad construction crew's campsite, but Slocum didn't think they had blazed this trail. It had the look of antiquity about it—and in spite of its age, it was clear of most vegetation. Whoever used it kept the path in good repair.

He hoped they did, at any rate. The paint stepped cautiously, and Slocum wasn't going to hurry it. It made him giddy trying to peer over the edge of the narrow rock ledge.

"They will kill us, John," moaned Consuela. "Do not let him force you down there. Fight him! He is a bastard! He is evil!"

"He's all that," said Slocum. "What plans did he have for me after the robbery?"

"What do you mean?" From the way she spoke, Slocum knew she had been privy to the devious workings of Rodriguez's mind. "He wanted nothing more than to have you plan the robbery."

"What would leaving my body behind do for him?" Slocum asked bluntly.

"The Federales would think . . ." The woman's voice trailed off. Slocum filled in the rest, now that he had an idea what Rodriguez had planned.

The Federales would think their gold shipment had been hijacked by robbers from north of the border. If Rodriguez had been able to find a wanted poster for Slocum to pass along to the authorities, so much the better. The soldiers would not be looking for Rodriguez—and he could slip off with the gold and leave his revolutionaries behind.

"Where was Rodriguez going after the theft?" Slocum asked.

"He likes Guaymas," she said in a small voice. "We would have a mansion overlooking the sea. It is lovely there, with no heat and sea breezes to cool you in the evening. And servants! We could have servants. How I miss them."

Slocum heaved a deep sigh. At last it was out in the open. Consuela had been part of Rodriguez's plan. Or had she? He couldn't see what she had gained from making love to him, other than a moment's stolen pleasure. There was no reason for Rodriguez to send her along on this suicide mission down the side of a deep canyon if she had completely acted out her role.

"Why did Rodriguez send you with me?" he asked.

"He knew about our night together. I do not know how. I did not tell him. His spies are everywhere."

"So this is your punishment?"

"It is my death. *Our* deaths."

"What's below?" Slocum wasn't sure he wanted to know. Still, it was always better knowing what danger you rode into so you could prepare for it, if he could do anything at all from this narrow path.

"The Yaqui," she said. "They hold their awful festivals on the floor of this canyon. It is their religious ground. No one enters who is not of their religion."

"I thought they were Catholics."

Consuela snorted in disgust. "The Jesuits taught them. They think the rest of us are pagans, but we do not do the terrible things they do. We do not nail someone to the cross every Pascua and consider it an honor to die there."

"Are there likely to be Yaquis on the canyon floor now?" Slocum didn't like the odds. Getting out of the canyon by following the river would be more hazardous than he'd anticipated. Yaqui villages were likely to be spotted along the water. And escaping with the gold looked more dangerous than just trying to get escape.

"Of course. And worse. They have *sierpas*!"

Slocum said nothing. He had no idea what a *sierpa* might be. When he didn't speak Consuela furnished the information.

"You stupid gringo. You laugh at the idea of giant meat-eaters in these canyons. But they are real! They eat and eat until they are large enough to slip into the sea to live. No one escapes them. No one!"

"Do the Yaquis control them? Are they like dogs that come at their whistle and fetch intruders?"

"You laugh. You will die! A *sierpa* will gnaw your bones and grow larger! And there are *coludos*, the seven-toed coyote with the long tail. Pray you do not see *un coludo*."

"Do they eat *sierpas*?" he asked, amused at Consuela's faith in mythological beasts.

"They are a sign of buried treasure—and where there is silver and gold, you will find the Yaquis. I am not sure whether it is better to die being ripped apart by a *sierpa* or to let a Yaqui capture us." The woman shuddered as if she had taken cold. The hot wind blowing from the bottom of the canyon turned Slocum's face into a sea of sweat.

"I've heard stories about them," said Slocum. "They punish their children by tying them to fences and lighting fires under their feet."

"*Sí*, it is true. They do that. They are brutal with their own—and intruders fare even worse. They tolerate no weakness. None!"

"Charming folks," said Slocum. He settled into the lurching pace set by his horse as the paint made its way down the steep trail. At mid-afternoon the *pistolero* in the lead called back. Slocum dismounted and forced his way past Consuela and three others to see what the fuss was about.

"*Mira*," said the bandito. He pointed to a spot not ten yards off the trail. Huge boulders had been ripped out of the sheer rock cliff and sent cascading to the canyon below.

"That's where the car hit," said Slocum. He wasn't sure if it was the first or second impact. For all their traveling, they hadn't made much progress. He craned his neck and stared up toward the rim where Rodriguez was waiting for them—or where the Federales were peering down in wonder at what had destroyed a section of railroad track so thoroughly. He saw nothing but the outjut of rock. The cliff might extend all the way to the sky.

"I'm going to check it out," said Slocum.

"No, John, it is foolish. What can you find? It is only a scar on the mountainside," said Consuela.

"How do I know what I'll find until I look?" Slocum began working his way across the rough face of the cliff, fingers strained, and his boot toes dug into dirt-filled pockets for purchase. He took a deep breath and swung over onto the flattened area beyond the harrowing route he had just traversed.

A large hunk of the mountain had been knocked free, but part of the railcar had been left behind. Slocum scooted on hands and knees to it and examined the piece. And under it he found a small brown leather bag that had been ripped open.

"Gold!" he called. "I found a bag of gold dust. It's spilled out the gold dust, though." The tattered pouch went inside his shirt. There was a little gold powder clinging to the inside of the leather. He stared at the gold streak on the ground and regretted not being able to sift through the dirt and get the rest of the dust.

Slocum started back and then found himself confused. He was dizzy and couldn't remember where he was.

In the distance he heard Consuela calling to him. He tried to speak and couldn't remember the words.

"It is the *chictura*. The Yaquis have placed a curse on him!" cried a pistolero.

Slocum sat down heavily and began to slide. He vaguely knew this would be fatal. He reached out and clung to a large rock. He stopped sliding. But he couldn't remember how to get back to Consuela. She was . . . somewhere.

"John, this direction. Come here. Come to me!"

He forced the mental fog away and concentrated on the woman's voice. Retracing his perilous path while not knowing what he was doing didn't bother him as much as the utter confusion. He had no idea where he was or how he'd gotten here.

"*Chictura*," muttered the men and backed away from him when he dropped to the rocky path at his horse's feet.

"He is all right now. He has fought it and won. He is a strong man, stronger than Yaqui witching," declared Consuela.

"What happened to me? I was over there, and I couldn't remember how to get back. I knew how, but it seemed wrong."

"The Yaquis curse those who enter their lands," Consuela said seriously. "The *chictura* causes disorientation. You cannot remember locations, even ones known to you all your life. It is a dangerous thing to forget where you have been in these canyons."

"You can die fast," he guessed. Slocum would have called any man a liar who'd said the Yaqui curse might be real, but he had experienced it himself.

"There are other curses," muttered a *pistolero* standing and staring at Slocum. "They are *brujos*. We should not continue. Let us return."

"You can go back. I'd rather not face Rodriguez," said Slocum. Any man returning to the canyon rim without the gold or a damned good reason for turning tail and running was likely to end up on the canyon floor fast. Rodriguez wasn't going to let petty superstition stand in his way to riches.

The *pistoleros* talked rapidly among themselves. They had to balance the threat of the Yaquis and their magical curses with the certain wrath of Jamie Rodriguez.

"We will go on," said the spokesman, "but we must do it quickly. We do not want to linger."

Slocum laughed without humor at this. He had to agree. The sooner he left the accursed Yaqui territory behind, the more sure he was to stay alive.

They continued down the steep, stony path. As they

rode, Slocum pulled out the leather bag and examined it carefully. At most, a dollar's worth of gold dust clung to the sack's rough interior. Slocum stashed it in his shirt pocket. He might need the bag later. With any luck—which had been lacking up till now—he would be able to fill it with the gold found at the bottom of the canyon.

The sun vanished quickly behind the high cliffs and plunged them into darkness by five o'clock. Slocum kept them moving along the trail. To be trapped on the narrow ledge all night was suicidal. If a horse balked or reared at a snake or other nocturnal animal, the horse would topple over the side. Even worse, it might take its rider with it.

They descended into the hot mist he had seen from above. The sky vanished by six o'clock, hidden by curtains of solid rock. By seven they reached the canyon floor and found the source of the liquid gushing Slocum had heard from so far above.

"Water your horses," he said, staring at the clear, cool water, "but don't let them bloat." He dropped to his knees and lifted the water to his lips. It had a bitter iron taste to it but the liquid soothed his parched throat and refreshed better than any whiskey.

"Where do we search for the armored car?" asked Consuela. "There is no way to know if we go left or right."

"At least those are our only options." Slocum considered the problem. As he'd ridden, he had tried to see where the car had crashed through the cottonwoods along the river. He hadn't seen anywhere that looked like a good place to start.

"I do not like this. I want to return," muttered a *pistolero*. "What can Rodriguez do to us that the Yaquis couldn't?"

That idea caught hold among the banditos. Slocum spoke up to keep them from deserting him.

"We split up. One group goes upriver and the other

goes down. That way we double our chance of finding the gold," he said. "And we only have to spend half as long in the canyon."

"This is good," said one *pistolero*, "but is it wise to split our forces in this way? Half of our force might not be able to fight off a Yaqui attack."

"We're not here to fight," Slocum said. "We're here to find the gold and then get the hell out."

This sentiment went over well with the men. They decided among themselves who was to accompany Slocum and Consuela and who was to go upriver. Slocum cursed. He had hoped to explore alone—or with just Consuela. That way he could have kept riding, and to hell with fetching the gold for Rodriguez.

Two men came with him and Consuela, and the other four rode off uneasily, following the stream. Slocum watched them vanish into the gloom. He let his horse drink a bit more before deciding to get moving.

"Keep a sharp lookout for the gold," he told her. "I'm going to be worrying about the Yaquis."

"*Bueno*," murmured one of the two *pistoleros* riding with them. "It is always good to be alert for them."

The words had barely slipped from the vaquero's lips when he slumped forward, dead. An arrow had buried itself in his back.

"Yaquis!" cried Consuela.

10

Slocum swung around smoothly, his hand going instinctively to his Colt Navy. He drew the six-shooter and fired. A Yaqui screeched like some evil spirit and tumbled from the cottonwood tree limb where he had been hidden. Slocum followed the *indio* to the ground, his sights on the fallen man.

"He's dead," Slocum said. "Any others around?

"None," whispered Consuela, barely loud enough to hear. "This is a bad omen. See his painted face? He is *curandero*."

"Their witch doctor?" asked Slocum. He didn't care if the dead man was a saint, as long as he was dead and stayed that way. Rising in his stirrups allowed him to look around the tiny clearing. The single killing shot hadn't brought down hordes of the Indians. He didn't like staying in the vicinity too long, though. Someone must have heard the shot. The high, close canyon walls turned the entire area into a funnel for sound. Anything happening along the canyon's length was instantly transmitted for miles.

"Not a *brujo*, not exactly," Consuela said. "He heals as well as puts curses on intruders."

"My curse is on him," Slocum said. "Let's find the gold."

They rode on for another few minutes, the *pistolero* with them muttering constantly.

"Will you be quiet?" Slocum demanded. "You'll bring them down on our necks if you keep up that chatter."

"I feel a ghost climbing my shoulders," the bandito said. The man jerked around as if he'd been stuck by a pin. His eyes turned wide and Slocum could smell the fear.

"There's nothing on your shoulder, be it a bug or a ghost," Slocum said in disgust. "You're working yourself up into a conniption fit, that's all."

"That is never all," Consuela said softly to him. "The Yaquis kill with dread. Those about to die can feel the ghost clambering up their bodies. I have seen it." Consuela sounded as if she believed such nonsense.

Slocum wasn't going to argue with her. He wanted to find the gold, put what he could away for himself, and then get rid of the frightened bodyguard sent by Rodriguez to keep an eye on him. Slocum didn't like prowling around in the Yaquis' territory any more than they wanted him here. And he was going to oblige their desire for privacy by hightailing it at the first chance.

He smiled slowly when he saw a tree that had been ripped out of the ground by the roots. Only one thing could have done that and left the area around it untouched. he followed the direction of the destruction and found the core of the armored car fetched up against the far side of the canyon.

"No," Consuela said, making a tiny retching noise. Slocum saw the reason for her discomfort. An arm poked out from under the steel cage—and it was obvious there was no body attached to it. A Federale had lost it during the descent, from the explosion, after the armored car started rolling along the canyon floor. When it had happened didn't matter to Slocum. The man was long dead and past any hope for succor.

"Watch the horses," he told her, knowing the *pistolero* caught up in fearing ghosts crawling all over him like squirrels in a tree wouldn't be much use. Slocum poked through the wreckage and found two large strongboxes riveted to a heavy plate.

"I'll need help getting this open," he said. His hand flashed to his six-shooter again when he heard noises in the undergrowth. Anger flooded over him when the other four *pistoleros* came into view, leading their horses.

"We did not find the gold soon, so we backtracked," their leader said. His eyes widened with greed when he saw that Slocum had found the armored railroad car.

Worse than letting the banditos haul the gold back to Rodriguez, Slocum saw no easy way of getting away from them. They outnumbered him five to one, and he still wasn't sure of Consuela's loyalty. She might sell him out at the drop of a hat.

He snorted in disgust. He was sure she would turn him over to Rodriguez if it was in her own best interests. Right now, though, she'd do what he told her because he might be the only one able to protect her from the Yaquis. The *pistoleros* all had a religious awe of the *indios* that surpassed ordinary fear.

"Help me get the strongboxes out of the wreck," he called to the five banditos. He noted that only three came to help; the other two stood guard, as much on him, as over the work to get the gold free.

They struggled to release the gold, using branches for levers, and rocks to break the locks. Almost an hour later, Slocum sat back and stared at the heavy boxes. Resting inside was enough gold to keep him happy for years.

"*Madre de Dios*," muttered Consuela. "There is a fortune here,"

"Reckon it's not too close to the six hundred pounds Rodriguez counted on," he said. "Can't be more than a hundred pounds. The Federales kept it locked up real good, though. I'm not sure we could have gotten it out of the strongboxes without shoving the damned car over the canyon rim." The brief but disastrous trip from the rim had done much to break through the steel protection the Federales had built around their shipment.

"How much is it worth?" Consuela asked.

Slocum did some quick ciphering in the dirt and smiled crookedly when he saw the answer. "Back in the U.S. this is worth almost $25,000. That's a good day's work, no matter how you cut it."

Slocum watched as the *pistoleros* started loading the gold onto a pair of the horses sent with them for the purpose. Fifty-pound loads on each horse wouldn't unbalance it on the trip back to the upper rim, he decided.

It would have been better to remain on the canyon floor and follow the river out.

For John Slocum, it would have been ideal

"You will now accompany us back, *El Jefe* wants you to join him," a bandito said, his hand resting on the twin pistols thrust into his belt. Slocum wondered if he could outshoot the five of them and decided he couldn't. He'd have to make his bid for freedom sometime before reaching the top of the mountain—a long time before that.

Slocum was glad they didn't disarm him, or just shoot him outright. Rodriguez must want a body of a freshly killed gringo badly for the *pistoleros* to let him stay alive all the way back to the summit.

Or was it something else? They glanced back frequently, as if the hounds of hell were nipping at their heels. Slocum didn't have any supernatural fear of the

Yaquis. They were men just like any other. They might know these canyons and paths better than he did, but the bullet he'd put in their *curandero* proved that they bled and died.

"He will die before we reach the top," said Consuela of the man who had accompanied them. The *pistolero* swatted at nonexistent bugs buzzing around his face. He jerked and jumped at the slightest sound. What was most worrisome was the way he waved his huge pistol around. Slocum thought he might open fire at shadows any instant.

"The dread death will claim him," Consuela said positively.

"He thinks he's got a ghost on his back?"

"The Yaqui *curandero* did it before he died. That is the only explanation."

"The only explanation is that he's working himself up into a state for nothing," scoffed Slocum.

"You forget quickly," Consuela said. "Do you not remember how you became confused and lost within a few feet from us?"

"These mountains are high," said Slocum. "A little less air in my lungs might have done it." He remembered times in the high Sierra Madres where he had gotten so dizzy he couldn't even stand. The passes there had seemed higher, though. the Bacatete Mountains hardly amounted to a fraction of the height of those he had explored in California and Nevada.

Consuela sniffed and turned from him. Slocum watched her and thought again how lovely she was—and how dangerous. Thinking of the two of them together meant only death at Rodriguez's hand.

Slocum started planning how to escape his captors. Shooting his way out wasn't going to work. The five banditos were too vigilant. Slocum amended that to "too scared." They started at ghosts.

"Do we have to climb the rim in the dark?" he asked. "It was dangerous enough coming down in daylight."

"We go now," the bandito's temporary leader said. "Remaining here is certain death."

"Aieee!" shrieked the man afflicted with the dreads. He batted at his shoulders and arms using his pistol. Slocum edged from him, thinking this might give enough diversion for him to make a break. It didn't. He felt a cold rifle muzzle in his spine.

"*Vamos*," the bandito behind him urged. They rode together to the base of the narrow trail winding up the cliff face to the rim.

"We might run into the Federales there," said Slocum. "They couldn't go past the break in the railroad tracks."

"They will fix the rails and go on," he was told. "Rodriguez would not want their other engine."

Slocum knew that Rodriquez would have killed the engineer and crew and slipped into the mountains to hide. When they reached the top the tracks might or might not be repaired. He worried more about where Rodriguez had camped. He'd have to see which way his captors insisted on herding him, then go in the opposite direction.

His paint had just put a hoof onto the steep upward trail when he heard a soft whooshing sound. He looked through the gloom and saw the lead rider straighten in his saddle. The *pistolero* looked around, then dropped his rifle and toppled from his horse.

Consuela, riding just behind the man, shrieked, "They come for us! Yaquis!"

The short arrow sticking from the man's chest confirmed her guess. But Slocum searched the low vegetation around the base of the trail and saw nothing to give him a good shot. The *pistoleros* weren't above shooting at bushes and wildly crying out in anger and fear.

Their rifles left foot-long tongues of flame in the air that seemed to hang forever. When they subsided, another had an arrow in his torso, a clean shot from the side that had gone through his chest and punctured both lungs. The bandito lay on the ground, drowning in his own blood.

"There's nothing we can do for him," Slocum said. He waited for the others to do the right thing. No one volunteered. "Do you want to leave him for the Yaquis?"

Still no one moved. Slocum drew his six-shooter and shot the man through the head. The man's expression changed from pain to fear to relief in the time it took for the Colt's report to finish echoing in the narrow canyon.

Eight had ridden down the path. Three were dead.

"You take the lead, Slocum," ordered the man behind him. Since he had a rifle trained on Slocum's spine, the command was obeyed. Slocum could think of worse places to be. The trail was narrow, and hiding places along it were few. Whoever brought up the rear had the most to fear from the Yaquis.

Consuela fell in behind him. "John, can we get back to the summit?"

"Three of us have already answered that question," he said. "I don't reckon on staying here any longer than I have to, but the trail is tricky in the dark."

He let his paint go at its own pace. When the trail turned really steep, he got off and led the animal, stumbling and lurching through the darkness. Slocum cursed the stupidity that required them to retrace their path in the dark.

"We can make it, can't we, John?" asked Consuela, frightened.

He didn't feel like playing nursemaid to her. He turned to tell her to be quiet when he heard a faint sound behind them on the trail. Pushing past her, he drew his Colt Navy.

"What's going on?" he asked.

"*Nada*," came the answer. He squeezed past the *pistolero*, checked on the man who thought he was possessed of a ghost, and then worked back past the two horses serving as pack animals.

"What is wrong?" asked the first *pistolero*.

"Look for yourself."

"José! Where is José? He is gone, vanished into the night!"

"The Yaquis got him," Slocum said brutally. "He didn't pay attention to what was sneaking up on us."

"They will kill us," moaned the bandito. "We are dead!"

"Sit here and keep telling yourself that. That'll give the rest of us time to get the hell away from here," Slocum said angrily. He pushed back to where his horse was enjoying the brief rest.

"He is gone?" asked Consuela. Fear had gone from her voice, replaced by resignation.

"I'd count him as dead," Slocum said. He hurried his horse along, not caring if the others kept up. He doubted the Yaquis would follow them all the way to the canyon rim. The loss of their *curandero* might have angered them, but it was a long way to the top. Even the need for revenge died out after a while.

Less than ten minutes later, he was taken by surprise when a boulder rose up in front of him. Slocum's reflexes were good, but surprise slowed him. He got his six-shooter clear of its holster, but the powerful arms circling his body caused him to drop the pistol. The Yaqui hissed in his ear and tried to pick him up off his feet.

Slocum fought with all his strength. If the *indio* got him off the rocky trail, that meant he'd be dangling over a precipice hundreds of feet above the canyon floor. All the Yaqui had to do then was let go.

Slocum grabbed hold of the Yaqui's belt and kept his balance. The Indian jerked and grunted in exertion trying to get Slocum to the edge of the trail.

Just as he felt his strength slipping away and the Yaqui prevailing, a shot rang out. Slocum winced. The report had come in his right ear, deafening him. Burning wadding even singed the side of his head. But the pressure around his shoulders vanished suddenly.

The Yaqui staggered away, then disappeared over the edge of the trail into the darkness without uttering a single sound. Slocum spun and grabbed the still-smoking six-shooter from Consuela's shaking hands. She might have blown his head off. Only luck had directed the bullet into the Indian.

"Thanks," he said. "You saved my hide that time."

"Get me out of here, John, Please," she begged.

"I hadn't thought any of them would have run ahead of us on the trail. I was wrong. They wanted to pick us off from behind—and from the front." He looked up and saw that they were less than a hundred yards from the top of the trail.

When he looked back, he wasn't pleased. The ghost-ridden *pistolero* was still struggling with his phantom burden next to the packhorses. But behind him walked only one man. The Yaquis had removed still another of their original band.

"Let's shake a leg," he said. "We can make it to the top in less than an hour if we hurry." He didn't have to urge Consuela. The other two followed briskly, much to Slocum's surprise.

They finally struggled to the rim and sank down to rest. Slocum's legs burned from the exertion. His horse let out an appreciative neigh. Consuela fell into his arms. The man going crazy with the Yaqui ghost haunting him gibbered and wandered around. The last *pistolero* stood just below the rim.

"Wait a minute," Slocum said, pushing Consuela to the side. "There's something wrong." He went to investigate. The man moved slightly but did not come up onto the railroad tracks when Slocum beckoned to him.

Slocum's Colt came quickly to hand. He fired into the shadows. The dark silhouette swayed and fell back down the trail.

"John! He was one of us!"

Slocum wasn't going to debate that point with her. He could make a clean break now and get away from the Yaquis, from Rodriguez, from all the trouble he'd found in the Bacatete Mountains.

"No, he wasn't," Slocum said. "He must have knifed the last man in the line and taken his place. He was going to cut our throats, too, but he made one mistake."

"He never showed his face. What gave him away?"

"Use your nose. The Yaquis reek of wild onion. Luckily the wind was blowing up from the canyon floor past him. I caught a whiff and knew something was wrong."

Slocum saw the chance to make his own break for freedom. For whatever reason, both packhorses had come up the trail unscathed. A hundred pounds of gold tempted Slocum, but he knew he couldn't travel fast enough weighted down with such metallic wealth. He wanted to get north of the Arizona border as fast as he could.

He swung up into the saddle and peered down at Consuela. "Take care," he told her. She clutched at his leg.

"John, wait. There's something you need to know."

"What?" he asked. He wasn't going to take her along. She'd made her bed with Rodriguez; let her lie in it.

"Yes, my darling Consuela, what is it you wish to tell Señor Slocum?" came Jaime Rodriguez's smooth voice.

Slocum looked up. Rodriguez and a dozen of his men blocked retreat down the railroad tracks toward Hermosilla. Looking over his shoulder, he saw another dozen uphill, making sure he couldn't go that way either. Once more he was trapped.

11

"This is all?" roared Jaime Rodriguez. "You only retrieved this pitiful trifle of gold?" The bandito leader shoved the bags holding the stolen gold from him in a gesture of disgust. "This is not worth the effort of destroying their train."

Slocum didn't remind the *pistolero* that the Federales had been blown up accidentally in their own train. The fire under the armored car had ignited whatever explosive had been aboard. It certainly wasn't any of their doing, not intentionally.

"You lost men going after it, too," said Slocum, not wanting to deal with Rodriguez any longer. The man was going to kill him whenever the moment was right. Slocum would just as soon have it out now. He had some small chance of getting his six-shooter out and gunning down Rodriguez before the other *pistoleros* cut him to bloody ribbons.

"None would have been lost had I gone after the gold," Rodriguez said haughtily.

Even though Consuela's hand on his arm cautioned

silence, Slocum spoke. "You weren't man enough to go down in that canyon. You knew the Yaquis were down there."

Rodriguez's anger boiled over. He reached for the brace of pistols stuck in his belt. Only the tormented shrieks from the man who thought the Yaqui ghosts were bedeviling him stopped Rodriguez.

The man screeched and began rolling on the ground. He pitched through the small campfire. Clothes on fire, he howled even louder. Slocum started for him, then stopped. Let Rodriguez deal with his own men. This one had gone crazy rather than face the threat posed by the Yaquis in the canyon.

Rodriguez drew his pistols, but they swiveled around and centered on the blazing man. Both guns barked. The man kicked twice and then died. The fires continued to burn, causing a stench of roasting meat to rise that sickened Slocum.

By the time the bandito leader turned back to Slocum, he saw that he was facing the man's steady Colt.

"Put away your weapon," grumbled Rodriguez. "We fight over nothing." He spat into the fire and caused a tiny hissing column of steam to rise. "There is not enough gold. Not enough by half."

Slocum didn't ask what he needed the gold for. Consuela had told him. It had been intended to finance a fancy hacienda on the seacoast for Jaime Rodriguez.

"The Federales came soon after you went down into the canyon," Rodriguez went on, "and repaired the tracks. They took possession of the engine and moved on. They will return. The mountains will become too hot for comfort, eh?"

"We should leave," Slocum agreed. If Rodriguez let them slip away into the vastness of the Bacatete Mountains, Slocum knew he could get away free. His usefulness dead might be behind him.

"If the revolution is to live, we need funds. Many pesos. Much gold. Much silver, eh?"

The *pistolero*'s tone caused Slocum to tense. But he could only go along with what Rodriguez was going to suggest.

"The Yaquis have much silver. We all know that. Who better to bring it to us than you, Señor Slocum? You are the expert at robbery, no?"

"I don't want any part of it," Slocum said. The cocking of six-shooters and rifles convinced him he did. He saw that he wouldn't get away without a dozen holes in his hide unless he agreed. "Except," he went on smoothly, "that I want a bigger share than before."

"You will receive your share of this gold when you return with the Yaquis' silver. That is a good plan."

"How many men go with me?"

"A few," Rodriguez said vaguely. "This is a night for rest. The day has been long."

Slocum looked up at the stars and guessed it was past midnight. Every muscle in his body ached, and he was on edge from playing the deadly cat-and-mouse games with Rodriguez. He didn't have to feign tiredness when he yawned and stretched.

"It is time to go to bed," Rodriguez said. He reached out and caught Consuela's arm and jerked her toward him. He planted a wet kiss on her lips, then turned and pulled her behind him. Slocum watched her go, her face a mask of pure terror. She knew what was going to happen, and no one was going to stop Rodriguez. Not now.

Four *pistoleros* prodded Slocum toward the far side of their camp. He dropped to his bedroll and started to roll over to go to sleep. One bandito reached for his six-shooter.

Slocum caught the man's thick wrist and squeezed hard until he yelped. "Nobody's taking my Colt," he said in a voice cold enough to chill steel.

"*El jefe* ordered it."

"Let *el jefe* come get it himself. If I'm going to rob the Yaquis of their silver, I need my gun. I can't fight them any other way."

The man withdrew, muttering to himself. Slocum knew the mention of the Yaquis had put the fear into this man. He had seen his comrade-in-arms die from the dread death.

Slocum lay back. The *pistoleros* circled him, keeping him in camp. Slocum smiled. It wouldn't be long before they started to nod off. When they did, he was going to make his bid for freedom. Three hours later, perhaps two hours before cold dawn broke in the Bacatete Mountains, the guards had drifted into a deep sleep.

Slocum rose and gathered his meager belongings. He wished he could make off with some of the gold he had brought up from the canyon floor, but Rodriguez had it on the far side of camp. Slocum wasn't going to risk his neck for a few pounds of gold, as much as he'd have liked to spend it. Life first, money next, he thought.

He walked up to the guard on the tethered horses. The sentry's head came up, startled at the bold approach. Anyone coming with this much confidence belonged here.

"Come to relieve you," Slocum said in a low voice.

"So soon?"

"So stay. I don't want to be here."

The guard grumbled and hurried off, not bothering to check the identity of the man replacing him. It took Slocum another five minutes to wander among the skittish horses and find his paint. He saddled the horse and made sure he didn't cause an undue stir as he rode out. Rodriguez's sentries were all asleep. So much for their revolutionary zeal. When Rodriguez found they'd allowed their captive gringo to escape, he'd flay them alive—or send them after the Yaquis' gold.

He went back down the mountainside, found the

railroad tracks, and started downhill. He didn't know if he would get to Hermosilla before noon, but he hoped he could. From there it wasn't a hard trip back to Arizona. He had unfinished business there.

The loud clicking of a horse's hooves behind him caused Slocum to swing about. He touched the rifle sheathed at his saddle, then decided his pistol was a better choice. Traveling was worse than swimming in ink. The darkness was almost impenetrable in spite of the faint light from the stars above.

"John!" came Consuela's voice drifting through the night. "Don't go without me! I need you!"

Slocum cursed. He shoved his Colt back into its soft leather holster, but he knew he ought to shoot her down. She was trouble—and she drew even more calamity like a lightning rod pulls down stormy death from the sky.

"How many of Rodriguez's men followed you?" he asked.

"None, John. I slipped away. They did not hear me. I swear it on my mother's grave!"

He cursed again. She had made enough noise to wake the dead. Not even Rodriguez's inattentive guards could have missed her departure from the camp. He pictured Rodriguez raging at them, then ordering the entire camp after Consuela.

"Go back to Rodriguez," he said brutally. "You belong together."

"He is different, changed. Ever since he got the idea of stealing the Federales' gold, he has been cruel and thoughtless."

Slocum doubted Rodriguez had ever been any other way. Consuela might be noticing it more. What woman wanted her lover sending her to her possible end at the bottom of a canyon filled with Yaquis and their strange brand of magic and death?

"Let's ride," he said. "You keep up or you get left." He put his heels to his paint. The horse dutifully started downhill, following the railroad tracks. Slocum hadn't ridden ten minutes when he heard the rumble from farther down the slope.

"John, a train is coming! What do we do?"

Slocum looked around and saw they had little choice. The railroad bed was too narrow for them to let the train pass. He had a gut feeling that they wouldn't be allowed to stand and watch. The train might be loaded with another company of Federales hunting for Rodriguez and his revolutionaries.

Turning back and going the way they'd come was suicidal. Rodriguez wouldn't be forgiving, no matter what he wanted from Slocum. He had to save face in front of his men. If they thought their *jefe* let his woman run off with a gringo, they'd probably shoot him in the back. Rodriguez had no choice but to kill both Slocum and Consuela de la Madrid when he caught them.

If he caught them, Slocum amended. There was still a choice, even if he didn't like it.

"We've got to go down the side of the mountain. Back into the canyon."

To his surprise, Consuela didn't seem as frightened at the prospect as she might have been. She smiled broadly and said, "I can help. I have a map."

"A map of what?"

"The canyon. Others that join it. We can escape Jaime using this map. He will never dare follow us."

"Where'd you get the map?" The rumble of the approaching train carried on the cold mountain air. Both the railroad tracks and the roar told Slocum the train was less than ten minutes away.

"I stole it from Jaime. It shows where the Yaqui silver mines are, but it also shows Yaqui paths leading west to Guaymas and north to Hermosilla."

"Let me see it."

"No! You must take me with you or I will not give it to you."

Slocum wasn't in a mood to argue. Consuela wasn't thinking straight, either. He could shoot her out of the saddle and take the map if it suited him. It took him several seconds to decide what to do about her.

"We've got to start down," he said with no real enthusiasm. The trail down the side of the mountain was steep and he knew it was littered with the bodies from their last foray. He didn't want to think of the Yaquis lying in wait along the narrow path.

Consuela chuckled and urged her horse to the brink. Slocum pressed his paint to go behind. He had gone less than twenty yards when he heard the straining engine on the tracks above. Soot and fiery cinders rained down. More interesting to Slocum was the volley of shots.

"What is it, John? Have they discovered us?"

"No," he said slowly. "If I could bet on this, I'd say the Federales saw Rodriguez and opened up on him. That ought to give us a clear trail to the bottom."

He didn't mention the Yaquis. Consuela had to know the danger ahead was as extreme as it was behind. He just hoped to hell she wasn't lying about the map. If they had to wander aimlessly in the Yaqui-infested canyon he doubted either of them would last long.

Slocum was exhausted by the time they reached the bottom of the trail. It had taken them five hours to make their way back down. His horse walked more confidently now, having made the trip twice before. The sun poked above the lofty peaks and turned the canyon bottom humid and scorching hot by ten A.M.

"I cannot go on, John," complained Consuela. "It is sweltering. I melt in this heat."

"It's probably a good idea to go to ground and wait for dark," Slocum agreed. "Thrashing around in broad daylight only invites the Yaquis to come to give us a once-over."

His hand brushed the ebony handle of his Colt as the

thought crossed his mind. They wouldn't be able to fight off even a small band of the *indios*. Stealth had to be their ally or they would surely be dead by sundown.

Slocum found a small cave in the canyon wall a few hundred yards from the base of the trail. Consuela fetched water as he fixed their bedrolls. He didn't like sleeping while the Yaquis were prowling outside, but he had little choice. He hadn't got much sleep the night before, and he desperately needed it now. And he didn't trust Consuela to stand guard. Better for both of them to sleep and hope Lady Luck favored them.

They ate stale trail rations and drank of the cool water Consuela had brought from the river. Only then did Slocum ask to see the map.

"It is here. I stole it from Jaime's pocket." Consuela pulled out a much-folded map and carefully spread it between them.

Her hand lingered on Slocum's as he reached for it.

"There will be time to study this later," she said. "I want to thank you for allowing me to accompany you. I know the risk you take."

Slocum wasn't going to argue the point. And he wasn't going to argue with the woman when she kissed him full on the lips. He was bone-tired, but Consuela had a special way of making him forget his aching muscles and bruised body.

She rolled atop him, her breasts crushing against his chest. The kiss deepened. Their tongues dashed back and forth, exploring hidden recesses and arousing both of them even more. Slocum felt Consuela's nimble fingers working on his shirt, his belt, his trousers. He returned the favor. He stripped off her blouse and exposed the twin mounds of her nut-colored breasts. Hard and taut on each was a dark nipple.

He bent and sucked one in, nibbling gently on it. Consuela stiffened with pleasure. She sighed, then gasped as he continued to work on the firm button. When he pressed his tongue hard into it, he felt the frenzied hammering of her heart.

"I need more, John," she cooed. "Give me more!"

Her fingers fumbled to get his trousers off his hips. He lifted himself off the bedroll just enough to let her get his pants down. Then he rolled and trapped her beneath him.

"So what do you do now?" she teased. "Could this be what you seek?" Consuela hiked up her skirts and exposed the moist triangle of fur between her thighs. Her legs parted incitingly to him. As if he didn't know what to do, she gripped his hardness and tugged him toward her.

"I want to play hide and seek," he said. "Let's start with the hiding part."

He levered himself forward, his hips driving his erection directly to its carnal target. Consuela gasped with delight when the purpled tip raked along her most intimate flesh. When he found the right spot, he stroked smoothly and buried himself balls deep.

A shiver of desire passed through him. She fit him like a glove. He was surrounded by clinging female flesh. For a few seconds he remained motionless, enjoying the sensations building in his loins. Consuela's hips bucked and twitched as she tried to get him to move.

Slocum wanted nothing more than to savor the moment. He was pulled into her with great force when she locked her heels behind his back. She arched up, lifting her trim buttocks off the cave floor.

He gripped the fleshy globes firmly, squeezing and kneading the round masses as if they were huge balls of warm, yielding dough. Consuela went crazy with desire. She squirmed and tried to get him to stroke back and forth. Slocum tormented her, drawing out both their sexual tensions to the breaking point.

"Move, damn your eyes," she sobbed out. "I need you so, John. Do it, do it to me. Fuck me!"

The sight of her breasts bobbing as she moved, the

feel of her body surrounding his, the asscheeks straining in his hands, everything robbed Slocum of his control. He began the slow, sure movements that lit the fires along his buried length. Friction mounted, and he had to stroke faster. His loins burned with need. He couldn't hold himself back much longer.

Consuela de la Madrid was too beautiful, and the way her inner muscles massaged him, he felt as if she were milking him of his seed. He began thrusting faster and faster. She squealed in glee and reached under her lifted rear. She found his dangling balls. Her fingertips stroked over them. Slocum couldn't hold back any longer.

He tried to rip her apart with every stroke. His ears buzzed and his breath came in sharp, ragged gusts. The fire in his loins erupted and spilled into the woman's yearning interior. Consuela arched her back even more and shrieked out her joy.

Good sense prevailed. Slocum bent forward and tried to smother her outcry with his lips. She moaned and moved away. He followed her, kissing and nipping both to prolong the sensations ripping through them and to keep her from bringing every Yaqui in Mexico down on their heads.

Slocum enjoyed their lovemaking but didn't want it to be the last thing he'd ever do.

"Oh, John, that was wonderful," she said. Her dark eyes looked up at him with adoration.

Slocum disengaged their tangled legs and arms and rolled onto his blanket. Consuela came into his arms. In a few minutes they were both sleeping peacefully.

Just past sundown Slocum awakened in a cold sweat from dreams of being tortured by the Yaquis.

12

Slocum came awake with his hand reaching for his six-shooter. His heart quieted when he realized he wasn't being tortured by *indios*, that it was a nightmare. He wiped the sweat form his forehead and sat up. Consuela still slept peacefully a foot from him. Slocum stretched and began to dress. The heat outside boiled into the cave, but the sun had passed the zenith and headed down. Checking his watch, Slocum saw that it was half past four o'clock.

"Time to be moving," he said, shaking Consuela awake. She stirred, a small, contented smile on her face. Her dark eyes opened and fixed on him.

"Right now. Can we not . . . wait?"

He knew what she wanted. Even though he desired her, too, there wasn't time. Although it had been just a dream, Slocum knew better than to ignore the threat posed by the Yaquis. This was their country, and he wanted to be out of it as fast as his horse could take him.

"We're leaving in ten minutes. First, let me look at the map." He picked up the folded sheet of paper and stared at it in the light entering the small cave mouth. Slowly, minute by minute, the light was dimming. Slocum had to turn the dilapidated map around several times before he got his bearings. The Bacatete Mountains were riddled with passes and canyons and tributaries to the Yaqui River he had never suspected.

Here and there on the map were tiny Xs showing where the Yaqui silver mines were located. He couldn't help himself. Slocum tried to figure out where the nearest one was. A few pounds of silver might make the entire trip to Mexico worthwhile.

He shook his head at the notion. Getting shot up in Hermosilla by the Arizona Ranger, the time with Jaime Rodriguez, the trip up and back into the Yaqui-infested canyon, nothing could pay him for that trouble. The knowledge that one of his cohorts in the Nogales bank robbery might have sold him out to Buck Johnson rankled, too. Even if he took all the money from the robbery, that wouldn't be payment enough for all he had endured.

Still, there had been compensations. He looked at Consuela. The woman was putting her blouse on. She saw his interest and turned coyly, giving him only the profile of her left breast. Chaste she wasn't. Slocum had to control his lust for her. Everything the woman did inspired him to more craving for her flesh.

"It looks to be a quick trip out of the canyon if we go downstream," he said. "Less than ten miles, then we're home free. We can cut to the west, find one of these low passes in the foothills, and then go due north to Hermosilla."

"*Bueno*," she said. "I do not want to stay too much longer—if you are no longer interested in me." She batter her long, dark eyelashes at him. Again Slocum felt the attraction and had to deny it. He didn't want his *cojones* nailed to some Yaqui door because he couldn't restrain himself.

"Later," he said. "When we get to Hermosilla."

"You promise?"

The grin he gave Consuela told the woman all she needed to know.

He finished getting his gear together, then packed Consuela's for the trip. He didn't like traveling at night, but they had no other alternative. This was the Yaquis' holy ground, and they knew it like the backs of their hands.

They rode downstream, toward a crossing canyon. From the map Slocum guessed it was less than ten miles distant. After two hours of easy travel, he began to worry. They ought to have passed the branching canyon by now. Another hour brought them to a crossroads. Two canyons met and formed a broad area around the river covered with summer grass and tall trees. He frowned as he studied the map. Nowhere did he see terrain recorded on it that looked like this.

"We're not lost, are we?" Consuela asked in concern. "This is not the place to blaze new trails."

"This isn't on the map," he said. Slocum turned it around, thinking he might have looked at it upside down. He didn't think so. The few peaks indicated on the map showed plainly—and he had not missed the canyon he needed to get him away from the Yaquis.

It simply hadn't been there.

"It's much darker," Consuela said. "Perhaps we have made a mistake?"

"Maybe," Slocum said. "Let's backtrack a ways and see if we can't find something we missed the first time."

An hour of backtracking showed only steep canyon walls. Slocum thought he saw the beginnings of another trail up the far side of the cliffs, but after following it for less than five minutes he found that it ended in a series of rock slides. At one time it might have given the Yaquis access to the far canyon rim, but not now.

"That was not the canyon. It is marked as *big*," said

Consuela. She gestured to show just how large it must be.

Slocum peered into the gloom. Blundering around in the dark wasn't much better than risking discovery during the daylight hours. He leaned forward in the saddle and thought hard. The map wasn't doing him a damned bit of good. If anything, it had led him astray. He could have done better on his own.

"We're going back," he said suddenly. "We might not take the trail back up to the side of the canyon with the railroad, but we need to be sure the way out's not farther up the canyon."

"We should rest," Consuela said uneasily. "The *indios* stir. I can feel it."

Slocum felt the hair rising on the back of *his* neck. He forced down the worry and concentrated on getting the hell out of the canyon.

"We've got to keep moving. If we stay in one spot, they're sure to find us."

"They kill in so many ways," muttered Consuela. "They can kill by dread, as the one with us before died."

Slocum snorted in disgust. The *pistolero* had talked himself to death. There hadn't been anything magical about that. Fear gnawed away at a man's guts faster than any other disease.

"Then there is death by sadness. The *tristiza*."

"Death comes from fear, not sadness," snapped Slocum. He didn't want the woman prattling on about the Yaquis and their supernatural curses. They died when he shot them. That was all that mattered.

"You do not know. How can you? You are only a gringo."

Slocum picked up the pace. He was becoming irritated with Consuela. She was lovely, and she was a hellion in bed, but other than this he got tired of her fast. Slocum cursed as they rode. What else could he expect from the woman? Don Diego might not be a kind father, but he had undoubtedly spoiled her with all the material things so few in Mexico had. Jaime Rodriguez wasn't the finest specimen of humanity in the country, but he had given her hope and the promise of a huge house on the seacoast by Guaymas.

Consuela de la Madrid had always been given the best. Living among the banditos could not have been easy for her—and Slocum wasn't going to let her take out her hardship on him.

They passed the spot where the trail led back up the cliff to the railroad. Slocum almost stopped and headed up it. He might be riding directly into Rodriguez's forces, but that might be better than running around like a chicken with its head cut off.

"They kill in many ways we cannot understand," she continued almost fifteen minutes later.

"I don't want to hear it." Slocum stopped and stood in his stirrups. The darkness was becoming absolute at the canyon floor. And the branching canyons didn't match those on the map. He had to believe Consuela had stolen a map and just assumed it was this canyon.

Another idea crossed his mind.

"How did you *actually* come by this map?" he asked. "You stole it from Rodriguez?"

"That is what happened. I saw him looking at it earlier. He told me I could not examine it. I grew suspicious. When he fell asleep, I slipped it from his pocket."

"Was it hard?"

"It was easy," Consuela boasted. "The edge of the map dangled over the edge of his vest pocket. He lay on his back, snoring loudly at the stars. I did not even have to disturb his crossed bandoliers to retrieve it!"

"He let you steal it," Slocum said in disgust. "This territory doesn't look a whit like what the map shows."

"It was not *that* easy to steal," protested Consuela. In

a lower voice she amended, "Perhaps it was. Perhaps he
has again used me. The *pato cojo*!"

Slocum held up his hand to silence the raging woman.
He'd heard a small noise, slight and possibly of no
importance. But the sixth sense that had kept him alive
throughout the war again warned him. Slocum pointed to
a small copse of cottonwoods near the river. Without
speaking, he walked his paint toward them. Puzzled,
Consuela followed more slowly.

"What is it?" she whispered after they were securely
hidden by the stand of trees.

"I don't know," Slocum admitted. He pulled his rifle
from its sheath and checked the magazine. It was full.
His Colt was similarly loaded. He wasn't even riding
with the hammer resting on an empty cylinder, now. He
needed the firepower. Of all the bad things that had
happened to him since coming into Mexico, Rodriguez
letting him keep his six-shooter was about the only good
bit of luck.

Slocum looked at Consuela. He wasn't sure if he
ought to include her on the positive or negative side
when it came to tallying up his luck. Without her, he
might have been able to slip away unnoticed. With her?
He didn't have a prayer.

Instinct rather than any audible sound caused him to
spin. As he turned, he levered a shell into the Winchester's chamber. He fired at the blackness hidden among
shadows at the edge of the cottonwood stand. An
ear-piercing shriek split the night as the Yaqui warrior
died.

"Damn," he said. "We might be surrounded. Stay on
your horse. Let me scout them out and see. If I'm not
back in five minutes, ride back for the trail leading to the
rim. Find Rodriguez."

"But no!" protested Consuela. "He will hurt me!"

"Not as much as the Yaquis will," Slocum said
grimly. He slipped into the night, walking as softly as

any Indian. He circled and quickly found two more of the hidden *indios*.

The rifle butt rose and fell, crushing one Yaqui's skull. The other whirled, knife flashing outward. Slocum danced away, lowered the rifle, and used the barrel to deflect another thrust. He couldn't fire the rifle and hope to hit the Yaqui at this close range. Instead, he dropped the weapon, grappled with the *indio* and brought his knee up hard into an exposed groin.

The Yaqui gasped, then crumpled bonelessly to the ground. Slocum pulled his own knife from its sheath at the small of his back and finished the chore. He picked up his rifle and continued the slow circuit around the small stand of trees.

More than a dozen Yaquis waited in ambush farther up the canyon. Following the river until he came to a crossing canyon was now out of the question. Slocum might finish off three Indians; taking on an entire tribe was too foolhardy to even consider.

He returned to where Consuela waited nervously. She held the reins to his paint in a trembling hand. He snatched them away and got into the saddle.

"Yaquis," he said. "An entire war party. We've got to get back down the canyon."

"We just came from that direction!"

"I know where we've been. I'm beginning to feel like a bug trapped in a matchbox."

Slocum walked his horse for a quarter mile, then urged it to a faster pace. He wanted to put as much distance between his back and those Yaqui warriors as he could.

He reined back when he heard horses ahead. They were still a mile or more from the narrow road leading to the canyon rim. Slocum had traveled it three times. Each time it had seemed a little narrower than the time before. But not now. He wished for it to be under his horse's hooves. The promise it held out seemed broader than the

Mississippi to a man wanting to get out of a deadly spot.

"John, more *indios*!"

He didn't need for Consuela to warn him. He had already spotted them. The Yaquis were good, he had to give them credit for that. Only one had momentarily silhouetted himself against the side of a chalky white cliff. The rest moved fitfully, imitating animals in the brush—or wind passing through the low vegetation. If he hadn't seen the one warrior he might have been fooled.

He dismounted and motioned for Consuela to do the same. He uprooted a few low shrubs and tied them behind their horses. Walking muffled the sounds of the hooves on the ground. The brush wiped out any trace of passage.

Skirting the war party, Slocum made his way slowly back down the canyon. Even if the other band was hot in pursuit, they'd miss their trail in the dark because of the little trick with the brush. To be sure, Slocum moved back to the riverbank the first chance he got. The gravel didn't hold footprints well. The rushing water erased what little spoor they left.

But they were exposed. Slocum kept a sharp lookout for almost an hour.

"Have we lost them?" asked Consuela. "I feel the ghost climbing my shoulder."

"They're around," Slocum said. "I don't know if they're looking for us in particular or just any intruders."

"Can we rest?"

Slocum found a secluded spot away from the riverbank for them to sit and calm down. The horses cropped at juicy grass and noisily watered themselves until Slocum put an end to it. He didn't want the animals bloating—and he didn't want them giving away their position.

He sat in silence and thought hard. What did the map mean? Rodriguez had allowed Consuela to steal it. Everything the woman said pointed to that. But why?

"Consuela, what else was Rodriguez talking about before he fell asleep?"

"Just the Yaqui silver. He thinks they have fantastic hoards of it nearby."

"Did he say he knew where?"

"No, but he might have. There was a certain gleam in his eye. You have noticed it?"

Slocum had. Whenever the *pistolero* spoke of gold or silver, that look of sheer greed lit up his eyes like jack-o'-lanterns. Slocum worked over this new bit of information and came to a conclusion he didn't like at all.

"He's used you," Slocum said. "And me. He wanted you to steal the map, he wanted you to join up with me, and he wanted me to follow the map. It was supposed to get us lost in the canyon."

"What would Jaime gain by that? He could have shot us at any time if he had wanted us dead. There is no need to let the Yaquis do his dirty work."

"He's using us as a decoy. He's got a location in mind. If we decoy the Yaquis away from it, that makes stealing their silver all the easier."

"Jaime followed us down the path?"

"He might know another way into the canyon. When we failed to bring back enough gold from the armored car, he decided to steal the Yaquis' silver."

"*Es un pendejo!*"

"He's using us as a cat's-paw. The Yaquis come for us and don't even think anyone else would be stupid enough to come onto their holy ground. That lets Rodriguez have a clean shot at robbing them."

Consuela muttered a stream of curses. Slocum marveled at how many different ways she cursed Rodriguez to hell. For a girl raised in a genteel hacienda, she had quite a mouth.

"We don't have to play into his hands. All we have to

do is escape the Yaquis, and Rodriguez might end up at the tip of their sharp little arrows."

"You make it sound simple. How will we do this thing?"

"We start now. We get to the trail and get up it. The Yaquis aren't too close behind. The darkness slows them just as it does us. They have to try to follow our spoor. All we have to do is keep moving—and doing it quietly."

"Let us start. I want to find Jaime and cut out his black heart with a dull knife!"

"You might have to wait in line," Slocum said. He got his sturdy paint moving slowly through the rushing river. The gurgling water drowned out most of the noise their horses made. Slocum began to think they could make it out of the canyon. He saw the foot of the trail ahead and hadn't spotted any more Yaqui warriors.

"There it is," he said to Consuela. "All we have to do—" He bit off the rest of his sentence.

The woman had been riding behind him. He saw no trace of her now. Consuela de la Madrid had vanished into thin air.

13

John Slocum looked in vain for any trace of the woman. Consuela de la Madrid had vanished as surely as if she had never existed. He fought down his rising panic. How had the Yaquis managed to snare her without giving any clue? He remembered all she had said about their diabolical magic. Thoughts of the giant animal spirit *sierpas* also returned to bedevil him. He forced that from his mind. He might have killed their *curandero*, but the man's spirit wasn't lingering in this canyon to kidnap unsuspecting women.

Slocum wanted to call out to Consuela, but he knew that would only draw unwanted attention.

Then he considered all that had happened. If the Yaquis had grabbed her while she rode along behind him, they knew he was here and they were just toying with him.

That didn't set well with Slocum. He wanted them to show themselves if they were out there.

He fastened his horse's reins to a low jacaranda bush and took his rifle and went hunting for *indios*. On foot he didn't have the speed he might have otherwise, but he had the advantage of being able to duck and hide if he came across any of them.

He found them less than ten minutes after he started hunting. And he saw their leader with Consuela.

The man was taller than the other Yaquis Slocum had seen. He sighted his Winchester on the Yaqui's head, then stopped. He couldn't rescue Consuela this way. The Yaqui chief was surrounded by more than a dozen armed braves. The shot would draw them to Slocum like buzzards to a rotting carcass. He settled down, secure that they hadn't discovered him and waited. It was going to be hard on Consuela, but he had no other choice.

"I am Cajeme," the chief said haughtily to his captive. "Do you know me?"

Consuela was too frightened to speak. Cajeme took her long, raven hair and jerked her head back. Her neck was taut and exposed to the sharp blade he held there.

"I . . . I understand," she said. "I know you. You fought against the French. You were friends with Governor Pesqueira."

"I was his friend," Cajeme said solemnly. "But I am no friend to his son José."

"My father knew the governor," Consuela said, pleading for her life. Slocum saw how the Yaqui had tied her hands. The leather thongs had been soaked in water and would tighten cruelly as they dried. Even now the slightest movement gave her intense pain. As she moved, agony washed across her lovely features.

"I spit on them. I spit on them all," Cajeme said. "Take her to the camp. We shall test her faith later."

Slocum's finger almost tightened on the trigger again. Good sense made him hold back. Cajeme was surrounded by too many warriors to defeat without an army at his back. They shoved Consuela toward her horse, but instead of putting her into the saddle, they looped a rope around her slender neck and tightened the noose until she choked. Slocum almost cried out in rage when a Yaqui vaulted into the saddle and started off at a brisk pace. Consuela was hard-pressed to keep from falling and being dragged by her neck.

"What of the gringo?" asked Cajeme.

"He must be halfway to the rim by now," answered another Yaqui. "He will find himself among the eagles, trying to fly—until he hits the ground!"

Cajeme nodded briskly. "Let us go to the camp. We have much to do to make amends for the *curandero*'s death."

Slocum knew that he had Lady Luck on his side. The Yaquis had laid an ambush for him on the trail. He had avoided it for the time, but when he didn't arrive, the warriors would report back to Cajeme. He had to rescue Consuela by then.

Slocum slipped silently into the night, keeping pace with the Yaquis as they moved through the sparse foliage and out to the river. He found the going harder since he had to stay in the vegetation, but he saw where they were headed. Although he fell behind, he arrived at their camp less than twenty minutes after Cajeme and the others.

He moved cautiously to get past the alert sentries patrolling the camp. When he got a good look at what went on in the secluded cove, his stomach began to churn and bile began to rise into his throat. He held down his gorge only by iron will. Throughout the war he had seen men blown apart. He had seen soldiers and parts of soldiers strewn around battlefields, and had never felt this sick.

The Yaquis had tortured eight men to death. One was pulled apart, his severed arms and legs placed on the ground in a cross under his limbless, lifeless torso. Another had been burned to death, one small burn at a time. He had endured thousands of the small blisters before dying in abject misery. Slocum read the true condition on the man's death mask.

Another had been buried up to his chin in the dirt, a sturdy cottonwood stick tied between his teeth to hold his lips open. Honey still lay on the ground where the Yaquis had poured it into his mouth for the ants to eat—along with the victim's guts.

"Who sends a woman to do a man's job?" demanded Cajeme. He began touching Consuela with the tip of his knife, poking into intimate places, then drawing it across exposed flesh to leave thin red lines of freshly opened wounds.

She whimpered like a whipped dog.

"Speak and the agony will end."

"You'll kill me!"

"All must die. That is man's lot. We suffer for the betrayal of Eve and the sheeplike trust of Adam."

Slocum remembered that the Yaqui had been taught by the Jesuits. He tried to think of what Consuela had said. All he could remember was her assertion that the Indians were fanatics—and that they considered the other Catholics in Mexico to be pawns of the devil, untrue to the faith because of their laxness in the constant pursuit of piety.

The way Cajeme used the knife on Consuela told Slocum the Yaqui chief would have made a fine Grand Inquisitor.

"Who sends you to spy on us?"

"Jaime Rodriguez!" she blurted. "The revolutionary who will free all Mexico!"

"I have never heard of this Rodriguez. Is there a *chone* for this Jaime Rodriguez?" he asked a brave.

The Yaqui beside the chief shook his head. He went to a small hut and came out with a doll the size of Slocum's hand. In fascination Slocum watched as Cajeme held the doll out to the firelight.

He saw that it was a crude representation of a human—but it had a human scalp.

"Is this the *chone* for Jaime Rodriguez? No, it is not,"

he said to Consuela, answering before she could blurt out a frenzied response. "This is a doll for children. I need to know more of Rodriguez before we fashion one for him."

"I'll tell you whatever I can! Ask!"

Cajeme seemed in no hurry to ask his questions or listen to Consuela's protests of innocence. He walked around the fire, heating the thick blade of his knife. When it glowed brightly, he brushed the red-hot blade against Consuela's left ear. She yelped in pain and tried to flinch away. She couldn't. He still held her hair firmly in his grip. Cajeme took no notice of the agony he had inflicted.

"Life is harsh in the Ocho Pueblos. The Bacatete Mountains give us little to support our families," he said. "We must teach our children to be hard."

"I know you tie little children to fenceposts and then light fires under their feet to make them obey," said Consuela, tears running down her face.

"It was done to me. I have done it to my children," said Cajeme. "It hardens us for survival. But you cannot understand that, you who were raised on a fine hacienda, who had servants to tend you." Cajeme spat into the fire, raising a tiny pillar of steam. "You probably had many fine and loyal Yaqui servants, no?"

Cajeme stepped away from Consuela. He pointed to the dead who had been tortured. "These are evidence that all men die," the Yaqui chief said. "Some deserved their fate. The *yori*, those who are not Yaqui, do not last long. Often less than an hour passes before the candle burning for them in heaven is extinguished." He stopped in front of the man who had been buried up to his chin and left for the voracious ants. Cajeme kicked at the skull. Slocum's finger tensed again on the rifle's trigger when the head rolled away. Ants had severed the flesh between head and body.

"This one is not *yori*. He was one of us."

"*Torocoyori*," grumbled several of the braves nearest Cajeme.

"Yes, he was a gray-faced Yaqui, a traitor. He lasted longest in his torture. It is only fitting because his crime was the greatest. He thought to sell us out to the Federales."

"Jaime fights the Federales. He is no friend to them! Neither am I!" cried Consuela, clutching at straws. Slocum saw she would do anything to end her misery. He saw from the set of Cajeme's face that only death would release her—and for a *yori* it wasn't likely to be a pleasant death.

"He fights the Federales," mused Cajeme. "I remember this *yori*. I remember him now."

"Then you know . . ." Consuela's voice trailed off when she saw the anger on Cajeme's face. It built like a mountain thunderstorm, then erupted with equal fury.

"He tries to rob my people of their gold and silver. He is a marauder, a bandito, a fool. He will die slowly when we catch him trying to rob us of our sacred silver!"

"I . . . I was trying to escape from Jaime," Consuela said. "A friend and I tried to get away. We were being held prisoners by him. He's evil!"

"He is a fool, and so is the man whom you call a friend. He rides into an ambush."

Slocum knew he had to work fast. Cajeme thought he was halfway up the trail now. When the bushwhackers reported that he had never ridden into their trap, Cajeme would have every Yaqui in the canyon out hunting for him. Without his horse, Slocum knew he was an easy target.

He smiled without humor. Astride the trusty paint, he wasn't much better off.

Slocum thought of slipping into the night, finding his horse, and riding like the wind to get away from Cajeme's vengeance. Then he looked into Consuela's face. The beauty that had drawn him was hidden under a mask of the purest fear. He couldn't leave her, no matter what he thought. Hell, he wasn't sure he could abandon any *yori* to the atrocities promised by the Yaqui chief.

Cajeme motioned to his braves. They came and dug shallow trenches under both of Consuela's feet. The trenches came together in a depression where they placed a pottery bowl.

"We will leave you to think of new lies," said Cajeme. "We will not return until the bowl is filled."

Consuela screamed as Cajeme dragged his knife down the outsides of her legs. Her blood trickled down, puddled beneath her heels, then flowed sluggishly down the tiny channels to drip into the bowl. The thirsty ground soaked up much of the blood. To eventually fill the bowl would drain the woman's body.

Cajeme seemed to know this—and made sure Consuela did, too.

"If this has not convinced you to speak truthfully, we know ways of letting the sun bake it from you."

"I'll tell you whatever you want. What do you want me to say?" Consuela trembled and shook. The intense emotion racking her body caused the blood to flow from her wounds even faster.

"When the bowl is filled, I shall make you drink it. Then we will talk again and you will speak the words I want to hear." Cajeme spun and stalked off. The braves with him left also, but a few sat at the edge of the clearing and watched.

Consuela whimpered and moaned as her blood dripped to the ground. Slocum knew he didn't have much time. The wounds on her legs were deep, and the woman would soon turn cold, as if she were freezing to death. The only consolation Slocum could take was that bleeding to death was a more merciful fate than others meted out to the Yaquis' enemies.

Slocum made a slow circuit of the clearing. The hut

had two Yaquis sleeping inside. Two others watched Consuela's torture.

He had little time to act. Consuela would die, the bushwhackers would report that he hadn't fallen into their trap, Cajeme might return. The pressure built on Slocum to do something. He forced himself to be cautious. If he hurried his attack, he'd join Consuela—and the *torocoyori* whose head now lay on the far side of the clearing where Cajeme had kicked it.

The two Yaquis crouched close together. Slocum cursed his bad luck. If one had been farther away, he could have taken one out, then the other. To get both at the same time without waking those inside the hut seemed impossible.

For once luck rode with Slocum. One Yaqui muttered something to the other, scratched himself, and then rose, vanishing into the darkness. Slocum heard the sounds of the *indio* pissing against a rock.

He moved as quickly as he could to reach the one still sitting and watching Consuela bleed to death. Slocum's knife made a quick circuit from left to right and opened a new grinning mouth below the Yaqui's natural one. Blood fountained out and was soaked up by the thirsty ground.

Slocum had no time to waste. He heard the other Yaqui returning. He hunched his shoulders and started past the Indian. The other blinked in surprise, expecting to see his friend. When Slocum got even with the Yaqui's shoulder, he acted. The knife flashed again, this time driving up and under the man's left armpit. The sharp blade found important arteries running from the heart and severed them with a single stroke.

He had to clamp his hand over the Yaqui's mouth to keep him from crying out. Slocum worried that the *indio* would never die. He kept kicking and thrashing about, even as Slocum twisted the knife in its wound, doing even more damage to the man's insides. He finally quieted and sank to the ground.

Slocum tiptoed to Consuela, who was moaning and crying. Her eyes widened in fear when he approached. Then she saw who he was.

"John!" she cried.

He tried to get his hand over her mouth to stifle the outburst and failed.

His name echoed up and down the canyon, loud enough to raise the dead. Slocum slashed at her bonds even as he heard the two Yaquis inside the hut stirring.

"Don't make a sound," he hissed. "We've got to get away."

"John!" she cried again. "Behind you!"

Slocum ducked and feinted to the right, then dived left. Two arrows whooshed through the air where his body would have been had he not dodged. He hit the dirt and rolled, finding his six-shooter.

He didn't want to fire, but he would be dead in a flash if he didn't. The Yaquis from inside the hut were already nocking arrows for a second try at his life. He fired and caught one in the throat. The *indio* gasped and sank to the ground, clutching his shattered neck.

The other loosed his arrow. Slocum winced as he felt it pin him to the ground. He jerked and his shirt ripped away; the arrow had missed the fleshy part of his arm and had only caught fabric.

He fired twice more, one shot hitting the remaining Yaqui in the chest. The *indio* stumbled but did not die. He nocked a third arrow.

Even worse, Slocum heard the alarm being raised in the direction of the main camp. Cajeme and the others would be back in a few seconds to investigate. When they found three dead friends, they wouldn't treat their murderer kindly.

Slocum knew the Yaquis didn't treat *any* intruder kindly. The proof of that lay dead all around him.

He fired a fourth time and caught the Yaqui in his right arm. Slocum hoped he had shattered the brave's elbow. That'd keep him out of action permanently.

"Save me, John. Don't let me die here. Not like this!"

Slocum rolled back to Consuela and savagely slashed at her bonds. The woman collapsed to the ground, unable to stand on her injured legs.

"You'll have to make it on your own. It's not going to do any good if we both die."

Slocum hated like hell leaving her to her own devices. He had no choice. Cajeme and a score of warriors boiled into the clearing. Slocum used the last bullet in the Colt to force them to cover. He scooped up his rifle and ran into the night.

It wouldn't be long before they came for him. He'd need all the firepower he could carry then.

14

Slocum couldn't outrun all Cajeme's braves. He ran until he began to breath hard, then looked around for a place to ambush a few of them. He needed to reduce the odds. From all that he had seen and heard, he wasn't going to scare off any of the braves.

Anyone who punished their children by putting their feet to fire wasn't going to fear death at a gringo's hand. It would be too clean and quick an end to truly fear.

A vital question flashed through Slocum's head: What *did* the Yaquis fear?

A slow grin spread over his face. Their *curandero* was entrusted with driving away the evil spirits that might inhabit their bodies. Consuela spoke fearfully of the *tristiza* and the *chictura*, but those fears had to originate with the Yaquis. They did not fear physical death, but they did have an acute sense of possession by spirits.

Their *curandero* cured the spirit as well as the body—and Slocum had killed him.

"*Sierpa*," mused Slocum. He didn't know how to imitate such a mythical beast, but he could only do his best.

He flopped behind a fallen log and reloaded his Colt. Satisfied with its charge, he pushed it back into his holster. Taking his rifle, he propped up a tall log, then draped it with his shirt. Moss and grass filled it out and gave a vaguely animal silhouette.

Slocum took a deep, steadying breath and then put his bold plan into action. He walked out in front of the crude apparition he had built and waited for the soft sounds of Yaqui feet against the ground to reach him. When he was sure at least three had started for him, he shouted at the top of his lungs, "*Sierpas!* They're after us! Run! *Sierpas!*"

He heard a collective gasp go up among the Yaquis. One fired an arrow at Slocum's shirt. It passed through harmlessly. Slocum roared like a hurt animal. The Yaqui didn't seem to notice it came from their prey and not from the direction of their mythical beast.

Slocum took another calming breath and began firing. Four Yaquis jerked and fell. A fifth clutched his leg and escaped back into the cottonwoods near the river. If there had been more, Slocum didn't know. He had reduced those after him and put the fear of the supernatural into at least one other.

He went from fallen Yaqui to Yaqui, cutting the throats of two of them; he had only winged them. He didn't like this cold-blooded killing. He had done too much like it when he had ridden with Quantrill's Raiders in Kansas, but it was necessary. He didn't want to end up a victim of the *indios'* torture.

And he still had to rescue Consuela.

Slocum took what ammunition he could from the fallen braves, retrieved his rifle, and fired twice into the night. Following the reports, he screamed, "*Sierpa!*" a final time for effect, then screeched as if the hounds of hell were gnawing at his leg.

"That ought to keep them running for a while," he said to himself with some satisfaction. Even this small enjoyment passed when he realized that Cajeme would muster his braves and send them after him once more. When they didn't find his body ripped and eaten by their *sierpas*, Cajeme would know his warriors had been tricked. Then the chase would be on in earnest.

He put his shirt back on, noting how accurate the frightened brave's arrow had been. If he'd worn the shirt, the arrow would have carved out his heart.

Slocum alternated between running and walking as fast as he could until he reached his paint. The animal was contentedly cropping grass and peered up at Slocum through half-closed eyes. The horse whinnied its pleasure at seeing him again. This passed quickly when Slocum jerked the reins around and vaulted into the saddle.

"Let's ride," he told the horse, patting its neck. The horse rebelled. It had expected to rest for the remainder of the night. Slocum urged the horse up the canyon.

He knew only one possible source of help for Consuela de la Madrid. He had to find Jaime Rodriguez and his band of *pistoleros*. The only question that bothered him was how to find Rodriguez. The bandit leader had gone out of his way to be sure Slocum and Consuela decoyed the Yaquis away from a silver mine.

"There's a mine above the Yaqui village," Slocum said to himself. "Rodriguez wanted us to go down the canyon and draw them off." He turned and looked back into the darkness toward the Yaqui encampment. He had no good feelings about returning there. But he knew Rodriguez wasn't going to be downriver. Another trail must come down from the canyon rim to the floor—and it was upriver from the Yaqui village.

Slocum closed his eyes and saw the victims of the Yaqui tortures. Consuela would suffer the same fate if he just kept on riding. He knew he couldn't do that to anyone, especially Consuela. He had to be careful, doubly so now that he had killed a handful of the braves.

Slocum headed back upriver. He left the stream and found the steep canyon wall. Hugging it, he made his way slowly through the darkness. He had to keep his horse from protesting several times when they came to rockfalls. Underbrush was denser here from spring runoff down the cliffs and made the going even harder.

Slocum was wound up tighter than a two-dollar watch by the time he came abreast of the Yaqui village. He saw their campfires and wondered if they were heating branding irons for their victims. Seldom had he seen such brutality. Life in the Bacatete Mountains couldn't be easy, but it didn't mean the *indios* had to be so harsh toward others who blundered into their domain.

Cajeme's voice rang out in the night. The Yaqui chief harangued his men. They let out occasional whoops. Slocum shuddered at what they might be celebrating. To have left Consuela as he did was a pity. If he didn't get help—and lots of it—she would definitely be dead.

He swallowed hard. He had to admit she might already have fallen victim to the Yaqui's heated knife or any of a dozen other diabolical tortures.

Slocum kept riding and passed the camp. He didn't relax. If anything, he became even edgier. The normal noises from wildlife in the canyon had quieted. Other humans passed him nearby. He thought it must be Rodriguez and his band, but he dared not take the chance. The Yaquis might be prowling around, even though he had taken off like a scalded dog in the opposite direction.

"There. We can go in there," came a voice he recognized. Jaime Rodriguez made little effort to hide his presence. Slocum wasn't sure if that was for the best or not.

He rode forward and found deep shadow to sit and watch. He had to be sure Rodriguez had enough men with him. Otherwise, Slocum admitted to himself, rescuing Consuela was out of the question. He didn't want to leave her, but he would. Fighting a battle lost from the start might have been the most honorable thing to do, but it wasn't the most sensible.

The *pistoleros* appeared on the canyon floor as if they simply popped into existence. Slocum knew they had come down another trail and didn't emerge from thin air. He waited until he identified Rodriguez before riding out.

"Rodriguez!" he called. "This is Slocum. They've got Consuela."

"What?" Rodriguez yelled and forced a rifle wielded by the man to his right into the air. "Do not fire, *joto*. You will bring the Yaquis down on our necks."

That caused a buzz among his men. Several edged back toward the hidden path, thinking they might have to beat a hasty retreat.

"They've got her, Rodriguez," Slocum repeated. "You've got to rescue her."

"Kill him with a knife," Rodriguez ordered when he saw Slocum. "There must be no sound when he dies."

"Don't," Slocum said. "I can bring them down on you before you get the job half done."

"Devil!"

"You're a fine one to call me names," said Slocum. He didn't mention finding out that they had been given a false map and had been intended to lead the Yaquis in the opposite direction. Rodriguez knew his robbery attempts were foiled. If Slocum did as he threatened, none of them might leave the canyon alive, much less rich beyond the dreams of Rodriguez's avarice.

"What do you want?"

"Rescue Consuela. Cajeme has her back in the village."

"Village? They have moved into the canyon?" Rodriguez cursed steadily for almost a minute before quieting. "We can do nothing against so many. We will go back and—"

"Try it and I start firing," Slocum threatened, his Colt

in his hand. "They're already looking for me. I've thrown them off the trail, but they can't be too far off."

"They would kill you, too," said Rodriguez. His uneasiness showed how he feared Cajeme and his *indio* band.

"I've come close a couple times tonight. What's another?"

"Consuela has been captured?" asked Rodriguez. He spoke only to delay Slocum and give himself time to think of a way of worming out of the tight fit.

"Get your men together and lead a full assault on the village. Most of the Yaquis are downriver looking for me. It'll be your only chance to get her back."

"Let us trade, Señor Slocum," Rodriguez said. "Her life cannot mean so much to you. Join us. The Yaqui silver mine is less than a mile from here. We raid it, take their silver, and escape. What good is Consuela? She is only a woman."

Slocum cocked the six-shooter and pointed it directly at Rodriguez's head. "You might not live long enough to worry about what the Yaquis would do to you."

"This is absurd," Rodriguez protested. He began considering the order to his men to gun Slocum down. They might still make a break for freedom and escape with their hires unperforated by Yaqui arrows.

"Five seconds, Rodriguez. That's all I'm giving you. Order the all-out attack on the village to get Consuela and you might live. You can overwhelm Cajeme and *then* take his silver. Sneaking around like weasels won't get you anything but dead."

Rodriguez swallowed and shifted uneasily in the saddle. "I should have risked cutting you down when you showed yourself. You have brought me only trouble and death."

"Take the death to the Yaquis. Show them who is *el jefe* in the Bacatete Mountains."

"*Arriba*," called Rodriguez to his men. Their apprehension grew. Slocum hoped they would obey their leader. If they didn't, it might be the smallest frontal assault in history—and the bloodiest since Pickett's Charge.

"We want the silver, *Jefe*," complained a lieutenant. "We do not want to fight the Yaquis. They will track us down wherever we go. And there are spirits in this canyon."

"That's only superstition," snapped Slocum. Then he remembered how he had deterred the bloodthirsty Yaquis, if only for a short while. "There aren't any ghosts here," he said, "but there are *sierpas*. You know what they are?"

Heads bobbed and the men began slipping their pistols from their belts.

"You're a tracker," Slocum said to Rodriguez. "Look at the ground."

"What?"

"In the direction of their silver mine," urged Slocum. He pointed up the canyon with his chin. Rodriguez got the idea and dismounted. Slocum figured the Yaquis' mine must be deeper in the canyon from the way Rodriguez peered into the night.

"Isn't that the track of a . . . of a *coludo*?" Slocum asked, struggling to remember the name of the oversized supernatural coyote Consuela had mentioned to him.

"A very big *coludo*, *si*," Rodriguez said. "There is a seven-toed print here. Their cache must be immense. The *coludo* only prowls near huge treasure!"

"There you have it. The Yaquis do have their silver here, and you can't get it without killing them all first," Slocum declared. He saw the play of greed overcoming fear on many of the *pistoleros*' faces. He needed to goad them into action. So much discussion might be attracting unwanted attention. The last thing he needed was to give Cajeme time to organize a defense.

In this canyon, it would be too easy to do. All Cajeme

had to do was to send a few warriors up onto the cliff
faces. From there they could shoot down into the mass of
any attacking force. Their arrows would be devastating,
no matter how Rodriguez and his men fired up at them.
Or they could roll rocks from above and either crush or
impede the attack. Defense was simple, attack difficult.

But Slocum didn't tell Rodriguez that all he wanted
was to get Consuela free. To hell with the *pistoleros* and
their leader. In the confusion Slocum hoped to be able to
slip away with the woman and leave Rodriguez to fight
the war he had done so much to avoid facing.

Someone let out a whoop and raced toward the Yaqui
village. Slocum might fault him for lack of good sense,
but the bandito gave the impetus for the others to follow.
Slocum waited for Rodriguez to get back in the saddle
before joining the full-scale attack.

"I should have killed you long ago. I did not need to
leave a gringo body for the Federales. Any buzzard meat
would have done. I should have killed you!" Rodriguez
cried.

"You might still get your chance to do that," Slocum
called to the *pistolero*, putting his heels into his paint's
sides. "Kill Cajeme, then come for me!"

He saw that this had inspired Rodriguez. The bandito
leader whooped and screeched and raced down the
riverbank into the village.

15

Slocum heard the shouts and knew that Rodriguez's men had rushed full-tilt through the Yaquis' camp. He hung back, keeping Rodriguez in front of him. He didn't put it past the bandito leader to shoot him in the back. Getting rid of Cajeme might be enough for Rodriguez, but Slocum doubted it. He had done too much to infuriate the *pistolero*. Trapping him in his own double-dealing plans had not put Rodriguez into a pleasant mood.

The rifle fire came in volleys. As the first wave of Rodriguez's men rode through the sleeping village, they stopped firing. The soft sound of arrows whistling through the air couldn't be heard over the pounding of horses' hooves. Slocum came riding up just as a second wave hit the Yaqui village.

He had thought the attack would take the Indians by surprise. It hadn't. As if they had been waiting for such a major invasion of their camp, they lined up and loosed their deadly arrows. Then they fell back and let another line of archers pick off the foolish *pistoleros*. Scattered rifle fire told that still other *indios* had more modern weapons to use against their invaders.

"*Ya basta!*" cried Rodriguez. He mustered his men into a fighting force. Again Slocum wondered at the man's ability. Rodriguez bounced back and forth from buffoon to an utter genius. Whatever skill he had as a general came to the fore now. If it hadn't, there wouldn't have been enough of his army left for a second attack.

Rodriguez led the attack. This time the Yaquis fell under the withering fire from the banditos' rifles and pistols. More bullets went wild than hit their target, but the explosive attack had its effect. It broke the Yaquis' spirit and sent them running into the darkness.

Cajeme howled and barked at his warriors like some demented wolf. But Slocum couldn't fault the man's bravery. He stood in the center of the encampment and swung his knife at every passing bandito.

The second attack took its told on Rodriguez's men. They reined to a halt at the edge of the village and dismounted. They got their rifles in line and fired, thinking they could do better from the ground. Sitting astride a horse and trying to hit a rapidly moving target was well nigh impossible. They did much better from prone and kneeling positions.

Slocum emptied his six-shooter into the Yaquis' ranks but seemed to fire only at smoke. Each vanished, and he wasn't sure he'd made a single clean hit.

"We have them now," gloated Rodriguez.

"Don't be so sure," Slocum told him. "They're like ghosts. They know the terrain, too. Get your men into a defensive position. I'm going scouting."

He wanted to find the small clearing where Consuela and the others had been tortured. Slocum was afraid he'd find her mangled, bloodied body and nothing more, but the point of this hazardous fight was to free her.

"Do not think to run off. We have much to settle, you and I."

"The silver mine will still be here. Just don't let a one of them stay alive," said Slocum, indicating the Yaquis.

He drew his knife and went hunting. He had barely left the edge of the village where Rodriguez had decided to make his stand when he felt rather than heard or saw a wave of death wash past him. Slocum dropped to his belly and waited. Scores of Yaquis passed him, arrows ready and knives drawn. He'd had no idea Cajeme commanded this many warriors. If he had, he would have left Consuela to her hideous fate.

Slocum let them go past, then hurried out from the village. He had no reason to return to help Rodriguez. The man had his army with him. Let them learn what it was like to be conquerors.

Slocum got onto his horse and started for the spot where he remembered the clearing to be. It wasn't far outside the main encampment. When he saw the numbers of guards posted around it, he skirted the area and went deeper into the canyon.

He left behind the masses of Yaquis intent on killing *yoris*. Slocum tried to circle and come on the clearing from a different direction but found himself going farther and farther up the canyon. On impulse, he turned and rode in the direction of the silver mine Rodriguez had been so intent on capturing.

Slocum stopped when he reached the mouth of the mine. Something was wrong. It took him several seconds to realize what it was. There was only silence from the Yaqui camp.

This spooked him worse than if the sounds of battle had continued long into the night. Damning himself for a fool, Slocum turned his paint back toward Rodriguez and his men, rode halfway to the village, and then dismounted. He left the paint again and advanced on foot.

The last hundred yards took him an eternity. He crawled on his belly, knife in his hand and alert for the slightest noise. The Yaquis had called in all their sentries.

He saw why. They had captured every last *pistolero* in Rodriguez's company. They had the men staked out on the ground and were working on them with knives. Some cried out in pain. Others didn't; Slocum saw that many had had their tongues cut out. Cajeme had trapped Rodriguez neatly.

Only then did Slocum realize the attack hadn't been a surprise because Cajeme's scouts had warned of Rodriguez's approach. The *pistolero* had not been as clever as he'd thought. he had come into the canyon to steal the Yaqui's silver. He might as well have been Hannibal riding his elephants over the Alps. Cajeme had known of his every movement and had triumphed.

Slocum tried counting the fallen Yaquis. He'd hoped to see more than a dozen dead. Four. That was all the loss the Yaquis had taken. Some walked with limps and others had crude bandages on arms and legs, but Rodriguez had failed to significantly hurt Cajeme's deadly band of warriors.

Slocum jumped when all the Yaquis began howling as Cajeme had done during the battle. They huddled by their campfires and passed around pungent cigarettes. The dense white smoke from the *macuchos* rose and blew across to where Slocum watched from his hiding place. The odor made his head spin. What it did to the Yaquis was even more pronounced. They settled down and stared into the distance.

The sun poked above the canyon rim before Slocum began to edge away from the camp. The *indios* celebrated with their magical cigarettes. Some dropped to all fours and dashed about like dogs. Others drew knives and took swipes at their prisoners. Whatever else would happen, Slocum didn't want to watch.

If he was going to find Consuela and get her free, there might not be a better time. The Yaqui victory celebration had debilitated them more than Rodriguez's attack.

Using every bit of his skill, Slocum inched away from the village. It took more than an hour to reach the small clearing where the torture usually occurred. The Yaqui guards had also smoked heavily and were asleep.

Slocum considered using the knife on their throats. He felt a rage that wouldn't die, but he restrained himself. Venting his wrath on them for all they'd done might work against him. A mistake now and he'd have more trouble than he could handle.

He moved until he was near the wooden post where Consuela hung limply. Slocum saw that the deep knife wounds on her legs had clotted over. The bowl that had been left to catch her blood was less than half full. Even so, she might have bled to death. Slocum knew that the dry earth could soak up considerable amounts of blood.

Twenty minutes passed as he lay and watched. He didn't want to risk revealing himself if the woman wasn't alive. Just as he was beginning to despair that she had died, Consuela twitched and moaned. Her eyes popped open but didn't focus. Her chapped, dried lips tried to form words. Nothing but a weak mewling came out.

She sank back into her coma. Slocum began crawling forward, keeping to the low grass and hoping he looked like wind blowing through the vegetation and nothing more.

He looked up. Cajeme had done terrible things to Consuela's body with his heated knife, but the wounds on her legs were the worst. He didn't want to think what the torture had done to her mind. He had seen strong men go mad after suffering less than Consuela had endured.

He reached up with his knife and slashed at the rawhide straps holding Consuela to the post. She fell forward to the ground, face down. He thanked his lucky stars that she didn't cry out. In her condition, she wasn't able to do more than moan softly.

Slocum used the pieces of rawhide to make a sling under her arms. Dragging her away without waking the drugged Yaquis proved easier than he had anticipated. Still, by the time he reached the relative safety of a stand of cottonwoods a hundred yards distant, he was exhausted.

He ripped part of Consuela's skirt away and dipped it in a small stream. He tied it over her lips. Her mouth worked eagerly on the water, sucking and wanting more.

"Stay quiet," he cautioned her.

"John?" The name came out muffled, unlike the last time, when she had brought down the legions of a Yaqui hell on him.

"Are you able to walk? I've looked you over and you don't seem to be too cut up."

"Weak."

"That's from loss of blood. If I support you, can you walk on your own? A little?"

She nodded. He gave her more water. She didn't gulp it down as he'd thought she might. She prudently sipped, then dipped the rag in the water and wiped her mouth.

"Feeling better," she said. "So cold, so weak."

"Let's go. Cajeme caught Rodriguez. He's busy with the torture. We've got to get away before they do a count and come up a few prisoners shy."

"Jaime?"

"I'll tell you all about it later," he said. Slocum put his arm around Consuela's shoulders and helped the woman. She grew stronger with each step, though she would have fallen a dozen times without his support.

He got to where he'd left his paint. The horse hadn't been disturbed. Too much had happened in the narrow canyon for a stray Yaqui scout to find the animal. He helped Consuela onto the horse and then led the way up the canyon. All the time he had spent kicking around the lower canyon, he'd never seen evidence of the Yaquis' path out. They had to use another road—and he thought it must leave near their silver mine.

"Mine," said Consuela, pointing. "That's a silver mine!"

"The one Rodriguez was looking for," Slocum said grimly. He left Consuela outside and went into the mine's mouth. The shaft had been hacked from the rock. He ran his hand over the walls. The sooty black rock told him how rich this mine was in silver tellurides. All the Yaquis had to do was drop the ore into a pot and cover the rock with sand. Heated overnight, droplets of pure silver would remain in the sand by morning.

"I'll be damned," he muttered when he saw the stacks of silver ingots on the floor. He dropped to his knees and did a quick count. "There must be four hundred pounds of silver here if there's an ounce. Rodriguez would have been filthy rich if he'd got this!"

Slocum left the mine shaft and saw that Consuela had dismounted. She gnawed at some of the jerky he'd had in his saddlebags. Wiping dirt and blood off her face, she watched him approach.

"We've got to get the hell out of here. It's not going to be long before Cajeme sends someone back here to watch over his silver. There's a king's ransom in there."

"So?" Consuela said. All greed had been driven from her. "Jaime was right. It won't do him any good, will it?"

"No," Slocum said.

"Can you rescue him? As you rescued me?"

Slocum shook his head. Riding back into that hell would be insane. The *macucho* smoked in celebration would have worn off, and the Yaquis would be their usual nasty selves again soon.

"We can take the silver or we can rescue Rodriguez. Which is it to be?" he asked, looking at her closely.

"I would prefer the rescue. No one deserves such a fate. John, you cannot understand the terror I felt while Cajeme tortured me."

"Compared to what he did to the others, that's

nothing." He closed his eyes and vividly saw the results of the other maimings as clearly as if they were in front of him again.

"Jaime, not the silver. That is my wish," she said. "If it cannot be, then let us leave now."

"With the silver?"

"Without. We can travel faster, since we have only the one horse. I would sooner die a clean death than be captured again."

"I'll see if I can get Rodriguez out," he said. He cursed himself for a fool, but he had to admit that Consuela's change affected him. She didn't seem the self-centered bitch any longer. She thought of others, even Jaime Rodriguez.

"I will not argue with you. Can I come and help?"

"Stay here. I'll try to do what I can. Rodriguez is probably dead or close to it. Cajeme has had him for hours." Slocum looked at the sun climbing in the sky. The day was hotter than he remembered from yesterday—but yesterday stretched to eternity in his memory. So much had happened, so many had died.

"You'll go on foot?"

"If I'm not back by sundown, get out of here. There's a chance I can get there and back in a couple of hours. That gives me a couple of hours to see to Rodriguez. I can't let you stay beyond that. It's too dangerous."

"Hurry back, John." She kissed him with a fervor that told him her strength was returning quickly. For all her wounds, Consuela's major injuries were psychic rather than physical.

"For more of that, I will," he said. He kissed her again and then started back toward the Yaqui village. Slocum couldn't believe he was doing this. He had come and gone too many times. Just one slip and he would be staked out in the hot sun with Rodriguez and his men.

It took more than an hour for him to reach the village. To his surprise, the Yaquis were still comatose from their celebration. The smokes were more potent than he'd thought. Slocum remembered what Cajeme had said about life being difficult for the Yaqui. An arduous life needed strong pleasures to help ease the pain.

Slocum wished he had a *macucho* to ease the pain of seeing Rodriguez and his men being tortured as they were. More than half were obviously dead. They did not stir when insects crawled over their eyes and into ears and mouths. A few made feeble protests. These Slocum studied to determine the strongest. Attempting to rescue all Rodriguez's men was impossible. A few might be able to escape if they had the chance.

Most had been staked spread-eagle on the ground. They were stripped naked, and the merciless sun burned their most intimate parts. At the edge of the clearing Rodriguez moaned and howled in pain. Slocum circled the area and crept up on the man.

His eyelids had been cut off. Rodriguez had gone blind soon after the sun came up.

"Rodriguez," Slocum whispered. "Are you able to fight?"

"Slocum? I am blind. They did terrible things to me."

"Can you fight?"

"*Sí*. Give me a pistol. I will shoot them down by instinct."

Slocum slit the man's bonds. "Crawl toward the sound of my voice. Don't move fast. I don't think anyone's watching, but I can't be sure." He waited until Rodriguez reached the cool shelter of a tall cottonwood before telling him, "Stay here for a few minutes. I'll free some of the others."

"How many?" asked Rodriguez.

"Not many," Slocum said, knowing what the *pistolero* meant. "Damned few, actually."

Rodriguez nodded, his blind eyes like white glass in his head. Slocum turned away, not able to look at him any longer. He crept back into the clearing and freed four others. They were the only ones strong enough to put up any fight; two had been blinded in the same fashion that had claimed Rodriguez's sight.

"I'll lead you to their horses. You'll have to take it from there," said Slocum.

"We will kill them. We cannot escape, Señor Slocum. We know it. Three are blind, two are unable to walk well from broken bones. We want only revenge. Jaime Rodriguez wants revenge!"

Slocum sucked in a deep breath, then let it out. "It'll help Consuela escape," he told Rodriguez.

"*Bueno*. I will do it for her. She did not deserve this nightmare."

Slocum saw that the Yaquis had changed Rodriguez's mind about greed and selfishness, too. It just seemed a damned shame he wouldn't live to enjoy a better life.

"There's their corral. Find rifles. Use them. I think Cajeme and his braves are still asleep."

"When they hear us in the corral, they will come in waves. We will kill them then," declared Rodriguez.

Slocum located the Yaquis' arsenal. His knife moved swiftly across a guard's throat. He loaded as many rifles as he could carry, stuffed his pockets with ammunition, and returned to Rodriguez.

"A rifle!" Rodriguez jerked it from Slocum's hands. "This will avenge my loss!"

"Help him," he told the two who could still see. He looked at them, silently asking if they wanted to escape with him. The hardness of their expressions told him they wanted revenge as badly as Rodriguez. He couldn't blame them. If the Yaquis had done to him what they had to the *pistoleros*, Slocum might be inclined to kill as many in retaliation as possible.

But he wanted to get free and nothing more.

"Take horses for Consuela. Spares will let you ride faster without tiring them." Rodriguez settled to the ground with his back to a corral post. He moved so that his rifle was aimed down a narrow ravine. Any *indios* trying to approach would be caught in his blind fire.

"*Buena suerte*," Slocum told Rodriguez, gripping the man's shoulder.

"*Vaya con Dios*," Rodriguez replied. He smiled crookedly. For the first time Slocum saw that the bandito's gold tooth had been cruelly yanked from his mouth. "Hurry. They are coming. I feel it in my gut."

Slocum jumped onto a sturdy pony and caught the hackamores of four more. He had plans for them.

He had barely reached the shelter of the cottonwoods along the river when he heard a volley of rifle shots. Then came a blast like a Gatling gun firing. He galloped off, knowing that Rodriguez would be able to fight off the Yaquis for only a few minutes.

At least the *pistolero* could die like a man.

16

"They got away? You freed them?" cried Consuela de la Madrid when she saw Slocum riding back, leading the tiny remuda of stolen horses. "What of Jaime?"

Slocum didn't want to tell her it was a futile effort on Rodriguez's part. On the other hand, he had to admire the man for trying to get revenge as he died. When there was only death on the horizon, try to take as many of your enemies with you as possible.

"He was in no condition to ride," Slocum said, skirting the truth. "He and three men volunteered to stay behind and hold off the Yaquis while we made our escape."

The rifle fire from the Yaqui village died down, then picked up again. Slocum guessed the *pistoleros* had reloaded their few rifles. They must be at the end of their ammunition. There were too many *indios* and not enough bullets.

"What do we do? Do we have to slip past them again?" The dread on Consuela's face bordered on sheer terror. She remembered all too well what Cajeme had done to her.

"The Yaquis have to get their silver out of the canyon some way. I didn't see any trace they took their treasure downriver."

"Why not?"

"No horse manure along the banks, no sign that the grass was regularly trampled by pack animals, no signs of foraging. That means they have to leave around here. My guess is that narrow ravine yonder leads to another canyon, and that leads to the railroad or the coast or somewhere they can trade their silver for food, rifles, ammo, the stuff they need to protect their land."

"That makes sense," she said. The listlessness had returned. Shock might do it. Slocum thought it was a major change in Consuela. She had become fatalistic. She had thought she was in control of her own destiny, and Cajeme had proven to her she wasn't.

"Help me load up two horses. There's no sense letting all that silver go to waste."

"It'll slow us down," she said, color coming to her cheeks. Again she almost panicked.

"If it slows us too much and they're on our trail, we simply leave the loaded horses and keep on riding. With spares to ride, we should be able to outrace any party hunting us."

"Let's not take long," Consuela said. Slocum smiled crookedly. He had to agree. He didn't want to spend the rest of his life in the land of the Yaqui.

They carried the silver ingots from the mine shaft and began loading them on the two horses Slocum had chosen for the task. More than twenty minutes passed while they hauled the silver. Slocum began to get a case of nerves. Consuela might be right. He might be letting greed get in the way of his good sense. Cajeme and his braves weren't to be trifled with. A single thought of those that had been tortured to death told him how true that was.

"Are we ready to leave?" Consuela asked. "I feel the weight of the world closing around me."

"There's one more thing I want from the mine." Slocum went back in and poked through the piles of supplies the Yaquis had stored here with their silver. They thought they were safe from thieves in the heart of their own territory. Slocum proved them wrong. He tore open a wooden case and pulled out a half-dozen sticks of dynamite and thrust them into a dirty burlap bag. He searched for another five minutes before he found the blasting caps and short lengths of black miner's safety fuse. These went into the burlap bag, too. He slung it over his back and left the mine.

"We're ready to go," he said, cinching down the last strap on the second horse and securing the bag with the dynamite. The animal shifted uneasily under its two-hundred-pound load of silver. The other horse, larger and stronger, waited patiently. Four hundred pounds of silver ingots were his.

If he could get out of the canyon and away from Cajeme.

"Jaime died bravely?" asked Consuela as they mounted.

"He did," Slocum said simply. The *pistolero* had died with a rifle in his hand rather than staked out in the hot sun, blinded and bedeviled by his enemies. "He might have found a better way to die, but he proved to me that he was an honorable man."

Slocum didn't like the way the *pistolero* had plotted to kill him and use his body as a decoy for the Federales. He didn't like the way Rodriguez had treated Consuela. He didn't like much of anything about the self-styled revolutionary and would-be dictator of Mexico, but he had died as good as any man could.

They rode down the narrow ravine, the sheer walls so close Slocum could reach out and touch jagged stone on either side. But he saw the evidence along the rocky trail that the Yaquis had used this path often. Scratches on the rock, piles of dried manure, bits of paraphernalia from their war dress littered the trail. No matter how careful they were, if they used the track often, they'd leave spoor.

He felt better than he had since he'd started ranging up and down the larger canyon with its small river and lush vegetation—and death behind every shrub.

"I cannot bear to be closed in like this, John," Consuela said uneasily. "Can we not ride faster?"

"I don't want to tire the horses. It's not hard to get tangled up in narrow quarters like this. Could you change from one horse to another?"

"No, it is too tight. I could barely pass the last boulder in the way."

They rode in silence for another hour. Then it was Slocum's turn to shift and turn and look behind them. He heard sounds echoing along the hot, cramped ravine. He put his heels to his paint's side and urged the horse to go at a faster clip. The animal responded. He'd have to see that the horse got all the oats it could eat when they reached a town worthy of mention.

Hermosilla might be large enough to tend a valiant horse properly. He'd certainly have enough silver to pay for the best.

If they got away from Cajeme. The sounds behind might be Yaquis on their trail. It might have been nothing more than nerves on his part, or wind blowing through the gash of rock in ways he didn't expect.

"They're after us, aren't they?" asked Consuela.

"I don't know," he admitted. "They might be. Rodriguez couldn't have held out longer than a few minutes after we entered this gorge. Cajeme might have rallied his troops for a small victory celebration—or he might have come looking for us straight away."

"How do we fight them? Do you have ammunition enough?"

Slocum shook his head. He didn't have enough for

more than a few minutes of intense fighting. And even if he did, they outnumbered him dozens to one. An arrow killed just as surely as a bullet. Scores—hundreds—of Yaquis firing their razor-edged arrows in his direction were more likely to take him out than he was to gun them all down. And he had ample evidence that many of the Yaqui braves were armed with rifles as good as his own.

"How much farther before we leave here?" she asked.

"Ride faster. Don't worry about tiring the horse," he ordered. An idea came to him. It was desperate, but he was increasingly sure that the Yaquis were not on their heels. Slocum couldn't kill them all; they couldn't outrun Cajeme's men if they were determined enough. And Slocum knew they would be.

That meant he had to make following so hard it'd take days to get back on the trail. There was only one way he could guarantee that. They had to get out of the ravine and into the open—and he had to get to the burlap bag with the dynamite.

"There, ahead," cried Consuela. "I see blue sky through the gap. The ravine is widening." She rode hard for the flash of sunlight in another, larger canyon. Slocum followed, even more grateful. The sounds from behind were definitely horses pounding on the rocky ground. The Yaquis wanted them—bad.

Slocum couldn't even begin to guess what Cajeme would do to a gringo and a *yori* who had killed his men, stolen his silver, and made a fool out of him. Whatever it was, Slocum knew it would be bloody, painful, and impossibly long before death came.

"Keep on riding," he called to Consuela. "I'll catch up."

"John, no!" She tried to wheel around. He waved her on. "I've lost Jaime. I don't want to lose you!"

"We're both dead unless you do as you're told. Get out of here fast. Ride north or east. I'll follow your trail. Now, damn it, ride!"

Consuela reluctantly obeyed. Slocum got into the burlap bag and pulled out the dynamite, blasting caps, and fuse. It had been a year or more since he'd done any mining, but he remembered well how to use the explosive. He bit down on the cap and crimped it to the fuse. He thrust the small but dangerous fulminate-of-mercury cap into the center of a bundle of three dynamite sticks.

It took him several minutes to clamber up the rocky slope and find the spot he wanted. Three sticks of dynamite might not be enough. He planted a second charge higher on the mountain. Then he lit the upper one, slid downhill to the second charge, lit this fuse, and took off like a cut cat. He hadn't reached the bottom of the slope when the first bundle of dynamite went off.

Rocks cascaded down the hill, showering him with dust and tiny pebbles that stung and slashed at his face and hands. The shock wave knocked him to his knees. He looked up and saw to his chagrin that a third charge would be needed to bring down a heavy ledge. He had blasted out the underpinning. Without a few sticks on top of the ledge, he could never close the pass.

An arrow whizzed past his head. He spun, his hand flashing to his six-shooter. He drew and fired. The Yaqui on horseback kept coming. It took Slocum three more carefully aimed shots to knock the *indio* from his horse. The war whoops from deeper in the ravine told Slocum he didn't have much time. The dead Yaqui on the ground had been their scout. The gunfire had told the main body of Cajeme's warriors that their prey wasn't far ahead.

Slocum worked frantically to fix the third bundle of dynamite. This would have to work, he knew. If it didn't, he was a dead man. He vowed to go down fighting as Jaime Rodriguez had done. To be captured by the Yaquis was to die a thousand times—slowly.

He scampered back up the slope and lit the fuse. He started to throw the bundle when debris kicked up around him. He didn't hear the bullets ricocheting until long after they had gone sailing off into space. Slocum turned and sat down on the slope and fired with measured cadence at the lead Yaqui.

The brave threw his hands up in the air and tumbled backward off his horse. Slocum winced as the second warrior kept coming, his horse's hooves kicking his fallen comrade to death.

Slocum stopped firing when he had only one round left. He looked at the dynamite in his hand and at the ledge above. He'd have to make a damned good throw to land the explosive on top of the rocky outcropping. Or he could use the last shot in his pistol to buy a few more minutes by shooting at the *indio* coming up the slope after him.

Slocum never hesitated. He pointed the pistol in the Yaqui's direction, stuck the fuse in front of the muzzle, and fired. The hot wadding and half-burned powder from the shot ignited the fuse. He got to his knees and heaved with all his might. The dynamite soared upward and landed on the ledge. Only then did he turn to face his attacker.

The shot had missed, even as it had lit the fuse. The Yaqui jumped from his horse and ran full-tilt for Slocum. Six-shooter empty, Slocum had only one choice. He waited, his hand resting on the hilt of the thick-bladed knife sheathed at the small of his back.

The Yaqui screamed and came in for the kill. He thought his opponent was unarmed.

Slocum dodged to the side, feinted, and spun, his right hand carrying the heavy knife. He drove the sharp point directly into the *indio*'s side. He felt inner organs yield. The Yaqui stiffened and tumbled back down the hill. Slocum made a frantic grab for his knife.

It stayed stuck in the Yaqui's side.

He looked up and saw death coming at him. A half-dozen Yaquis rode quickly to take the place of the ones he had killed. At their head rode Cajeme, tall, proud, and like an arrogant ruler of an entire kingdom. A sneer marred his face. Slocum knew he'd get no mercy from this man.

Just as Cajeme raised his bow to shoot, the dynamite exploded. The ground shook, throwing Slocum off his feet. He tumbled head over heels down the slope. He tried to roll away from the Yaquis. Cajeme might have fired. He might have missed. Slocum never knew. Tons of mountain came crashing down. The ledge had released its ponderous load.

Slocum coughed and choked and tried to sit up. He couldn't. He rubbed the grit from his eyes and blew his nose until he could breathe again. Rolling onto his side and then coming to hands and knees was the only way he could stand.

A smile cracked through the dusty mask on his face when he saw how thoroughly he had stoppered the ravine. He had faced the entire Yaqui nation and had won.

17

Slocum dusted himself off and simply stared at the huge plug of rock bottling up the Yaquis. He felt a great deal of satisfaction, but no real victory. Too many had died—and for what?

Jaime Rodriguez had fancied himself a revolutionary. Slocum thought he was more of a greedy opportunist than someone to overthrow Porfirio Díaz's tyranny. Whichever Rodriguez had truly been, he had died a messy death at the hands of Cajeme and his torturers. Only a final moment of triumph had been given the man. Slocum hoped Rodriguez had killed many *indios* before they got to him.

Slocum started on foot to retrieve his horse. The animal had bolted at the explosions and had run a good half mile before slowing and finding a patch of grass to crop. Of Consuela de la Madrid he saw no sign. She had ridden like the very wind, as he'd told her. He swung up into the saddle and gratefully settled down. Walking in his old boots wasn't Slocum's favorite exercise.

"Let's find Consuela and our silver," he told the

horse, patting it on the neck. "You're going to end up the fattest paint this side of the Rio Grande when we get back to Hermosilla. You're going to get grain and treatment fit for a thoroughbred."

The horse craned its neck around and stared at him from one gimlet eye, as if accusing him of lying. Slocum laughed. The day hadn't started well, but it had improved steadily. He doubted the Yaquis would be able to get over the rockfall before sundown. By then he intended to be long gone from the Bacatete Mountains. No matter what vengeance burned in Cajeme and his braves, they weren't going to find it easy to get revenge on John Slocum.

He'd ridden almost an hour when he came to a crossing canyon. He got down and looked for some sign that Consuela had turned here, as he'd told her. The canyon went east. He found cut grass where at least three horses had trampled through. He smiled. They were unshod Yaqui horses. Two were carrying heavy loads: silver.

Slocum rode faster, not even bothering to hide the trail. Speed counted for more than stealth now. He wanted miles and miles between him and the Yaqui stronghold and the horrors it held. That would serve him better than wasting time trying to decoy them off his trail. As dog tired as Slocum was, he wasn't sure he could do a decent job of covering his tracks.

Just before sundown he saw a small group of horses ahead. Slocum picked up the pace and overtook Consuela as the sky exploded in a welter of bright pinks and oranges intermixed with grays.

"John!" she cried when she saw him. "I thought they'd gotten you!"

He heard real concern in her voice. He dismounted and went to her. Their arms circled one another's dusty bodies and they kissed. Slocum pushed away after a satisfying kiss.

"We're both filthy and sore and trail-weary. I hear a river running over there."

Consuela turned and cocked her head. From the delighted look on her face, she hadn't heard the water. The notion of a bath appealed to her greatly.

"Let's go," he said, taking her hand.

"But the horses. We should unload them."

Slocum took a few minutes to drop the heavy silver to the ground. He made sure the horses were tethered but able to crop at the lush grass growing in the shade of trees nearby. Then he turned and looked for the lovely Consuela.

His heart jumped into his throat. She was gone. Then he heard a contented splashing from the direction of the river. He shucked off his duster and waistcoat and by the time he reached the riverbank, had his gunbelt unfastened. He dropped it on top of his shirt and quickly added his boots to the pile.

The water looked cool, fresh, and inviting—and Consuela was already in the crisply flowing current.

He stared at her for a moment in the light of the setting sun. Her breasts moved just under the water's surface, brown and firm and tempting. She tossed her head back to get the wet, dark hair from her eyes. She looked like a sea nymph.

When she spoke, she had the voice of a Siren.

"Join me, John."

Slocum didn't have to be asked twice.

He slipped into the cold water and let it wash away the aches in his body. Then he took Consuela in his arms and let her wash away the aches of his soul.

He felt the warmth of her body pressing into his body. When she lifted a leg and curled it around his waist, his loins began to stir. She stroked over his lank black hair and laughed.

"What is this rising from the depths? Can it be a monster?"

"A *sierpa*," he assured her. "It's eaten all it can on the land and now is hunting through the water."

"And I was afraid of the *sierpas*. No longer." She grabbed his firm length and tugged gently on it. Slocum let himself float upward. They rolled over and over in the water, neither interested in staying on top too long.

When they came to rest again, both had their feet on the shallow bottom—and Slocum's fleshy shaft was fully erect. Consuela peered down through the water and saw the hooded giant. She leaned back, letting him support her around the waist. Her brown thighs parted and drifted up on either side of his body.

Slocum moved forward, finding the woman's inviting nether lips. She splashed a little, then moved closer. Her legs tightened around his waist and they slid together easily.

Slocum murmured in joy. Warmth flooded through him when he entered her. She surrounded him totally, her warm sheath of female flesh clutching at his length with a startling tenacity. He didn't know what she was doing, but it felt as if a hand inside a velvet glove was squeezing and relaxing along his entire lusty shaft.

"We're alive, John," she said, licking and biting at his ear. "We got away alive!"

"I noticed," he said. He cupped her buttocks and bounced her gently, the water supporting her. As the waves began catching her body and lifting, she slid off his cock. He pushed her back down forcefully. The up and down motion in the water caused him to moan in pleasure.

"You feel so good in me. I'm shaking. I can't help it. My insides have turned to molasses."

"So warm and tight," he muttered as he continued to enjoy her. She moved up close enough again for him to kiss her. Her naked wet breasts crushed into his chest.

Somewhere in the up and down motion, Slocum slipped on the river rocks. They went over together,

Consuela clinging to him. Slocum managed to keep inside the woman as they sloshed around. Somehow Slocum kept up the in-and-out motion. This drove Consuela crazy with need.

She shrieked and moaned and sighed and clawed at his back. Slocum got into shallower water and rose above the woman. Half submerged, she lifted her legs high into the air. Having the leverage he needed, he began thrusting powerfully in and out of her until they both burned with desire.

"More, John, give me more. I need more!" she cried.

He gave it to her. He was tired from the battles with Rodriguez and the Yaquis and the long ride on the trail and loading so much silver—and he moved as if he had been resting for a week for this moment. Water frothed and churned around them. Consuela lifted her legs even higher, hooking them over Slocum's shoulders. He bent her double with every inward thrust.

And then the warm feelings in his balls turned hotter. He began to boil and churn inside. He tried to hold back. He wanted the sensations to last forever. The fierce tide of his come blasted forth into the yearning woman.

Consuela gasped and arched her back. Slocum wasn't sure if it was the touch of his seed or she had reached the point of no return independently. It didn't matter. Locked together, they both rode the storm winds of their passion until there was nothing left in either of them.

Slocum collapsed and rolled into the river beside Consuela. She reached out for him and he was there. They kissed again, then began stroking over each other's body, exploring and finding wondrous new places that excited both of them anew.

It was past moonrise before they made camp and fixed a simple dinner from Slocum's trail rations. They fell asleep under a single blanket, arms and legs tangled together after another bout of passionate lovemaking.

* * *

Slocum knew something was wrong by midday. Consuela hadn't spoken much when they'd risen that morning. If anything, she seemed to avoid him. The ride north toward Hermosilla had taken them across the railroad tracks twice. Slocum knew they were getting near the town, even though he couldn't see it yet.

"What is it?" he finally asked her. "You've been moody all day long."

Consuela didn't answer immediately. "I've been trying to think," she said after a long silence. "It is not easy putting my feelings into words."

"Try," he said. Slocum knew what was coming. In a way, it came as a relief. He enjoyed Consuela's company. In bed she was a hellion. But they came from different worlds. She hadn't belonged in Jaime Rodriguez's revolutionary band. She fit in more with his grandiose notion of a fine seaside hacienda in Guaymas.

"I must return to my papa's hacienda. He thinks I have been kidnapped."

"From all you've said, he didn't treat you well. He even raped you."

"That is so. He is not a good man, but he is all the family I have."

"It can be different," he started.

"No, John, not with us. We are not meant to be together longer than we have been."

"I wasn't going to suggest that. I've got business to attend to north of the border. You're better off staying in Mexico, at least until that's behind me. Maybe even after it's done." His thoughts turned to Ogelvie, Ballard, and Delling—and Arizona Ranger Buck Johnson.

"What then?"

He saw he had her undivided attention. In her world, there was only family. Beyond that was a strange and unexplored region she couldn't venture into, even in her dreams.

"Half the silver is yours. Two hundred pounds will buy you a nice place of your own and keep it running."

"You will give me half the silver?" The idea astounded her.

"Don't you think you've earned it?"

"*Pues, sí*," she said.

"You earned it," he said flatly. "For all you've been through, maybe you deserve all the silver."

"You would give me *all* the silver?"

"I'm generous, not stupid," he said, grinning. "Take half and make a good, decent life for yourself. If not in Hermosilla, go to Guaymas and buy a house looking out over the sea, just as you and Rodriguez had planned to do."

"That would be nice. But without Jaime, what is the use?"

"Then go to Mexico City. There are places to go where you can keep away from Don Diego."

"Mexico does not look favorably upon unmarried women," she said.

"So lie. Tell everyone you're a rich widow," he told her. "Hire servants. Find yourself a good man—but don't let anyone hoodoo you out of the silver."

She laughed. Slocum thought of silver bells ringing. "You make much sense, John. Perhaps Mexico and its ways are not for me any longer. I have always wanted to see San Luis in California. Do you think they would take one such as I?"

"And what kind of person is Consuela de la Madrid?" he asked.

"A rich, lonely widow," she said. She laughed heartily at this new appraisal.

"A rich, *lovely* widow," Slocum corrected. He reined to a halt beside her and bent over to kiss her.

"Our trails must part here," she said sadly. "If you come to California, look for me."

"I will. It might be a while."

"Your business in Arizona," she said, knowing what he had to do.

Slocum's thoughts turned from Consuela and went back to his former partners in the bank robbery. One of them had put Buck Johnson on his trail. He wanted to find out who—and mete out a bit of deserved justice to the son of a bitch.

18

The stolen Yaqui horse had stepped in a snake's hole and broken its leg a few miles outside Hermosilla. Slocum had replaced it with two mules, slower moving but much stronger and more dependable for carrying his two hundred pounds of silver through the fiery Sonora Desert. The closer he got to the U.S. border, the edgier he got.

He didn't think he had much to worry over. It had been well nigh a month since he'd hightailed it south from Nogales. The bank robbery would have been forgotten, or at least replaced in people's minds with something more immediate. But he couldn't get the damned Arizona Ranger out of his mind.

Buck Johnson was like a cat with nine lives. Slocum figured he had taken six or seven of them himself—and the Ranger kept on coming. Jaime Rodriguez and his men should have finished off the elusive lawman and they hadn't. Slocum had a faint hope that the Federales might have left Johnson face-down on the desert somewhere, but he doubted it. The silver-tongued Ranger had sweet-talked them into going after him in the Bacatete Mountains. He wouldn't end up dead through any mistake in judgment.

Buck Johnson ought to be back on patrol in Arizona Territory. Coming into the region leading two mules wobbling under a load of silver would do more than interest the lawman.

Slocum saw mountains in the distance and knew he had crossed the border. He began looking for a spot to bury the silver. He had business to take care of. Then he could think about moving the treasure into safer quarters.

He found a spot at the foot of a rocky hill. He took good bearings and began digging. He wished he had bought a shovel back in Hermosilla. Slocum smiled, remembering how good the time had been in the sleepy Mexican town. He had lavished every luxury possible on his trusty paint. The horse deserved it. Then he had seen to his own needs. The only thing he didn't indulge in was a woman.

Several of the whores had called him *joto* because he wanted nothing to do with them, but his basic needs had been met for some time—and the memory of Consuela de la Madrid still lingered. None of the women in Hermosilla came close to matching her fire or beauty.

Slocum rubbed his aching back as he pushed the last of the fine sand over the hidden silver ingots. He had kept one ingot back for traveling expenses. It might take him a spell to return for the Yaqui silver, but he would sooner or later. He just hoped a storm didn't blow up and push the sand off his treasure in the meantime.

The hot sun beat down as he rode slowly west to Nogales. He kept his hat brim pulled down when he sighted the town. Slocum didn't look around much as he went directly to the Green Frog Cafe and dismounted. He had worked up a powerful hunger on the trail. Burying silver had given him quite an appetite for real food, too.

Belly full and hunger sated, Slocum left the cafe an hour later and went looking for a saloon. He slowed in front of a rickety shack with an Arizona sunburst emblem on the door. This was where he'd most likely find Buck Johnson. Slocum loosened the thong on the hammer of his Colt and went to the door. He took a deep breath, then went in.

The dank coolness wrapped him up like a blanket. He squinted, trying to see into the gloom. A man sat behind a desk, laboriously working on a stack of papers.

The first thing Slocum looked for when he could see better was the wall where the Rangers kept their wanted posters.

"Can I help you, mister?" asked the Ranger behind the desk.

"Looking for Buck Johnson. Is he around?"

"Naw, he's out serving process. Won't be back for a week or longer. Can I do something for you?"

"He's an old friend. I was just passing through Nogales and thought I'd look him up."

"Sorry you missed him. Like I said, he won't be back for at least a week. Can I tell him who was lookin' for him?"

"It doesn't matter much," Slocum said.

"Buck can use some cheerin' up 'bout now," the Ranger said. "He's been laid up almost two weeks ever since he got back from Mexico."

"You don't say?"

"Got shot up by a bunch of wild men. Revolutionaries, to hear Buck tell it. I suspect he was out whorin' and some jealous husband came after him."

"That's Buck, all right," Slocum said. "No lasting damage to him?"

"Not a bit of it. I swear, he's the luckiest man I ever saw. He could walk barefoot through hell and not even get a blister."

Slocum started to ask about the bank robbery but held

his tongue. The deputy might get suspicious over too many questions.

"I'll be back this way in a couple of weeks," Slocum lied. "I'll look in on you then."

"He ought to be here." The Ranger had already lost interest. Criminals didn't saunter into his office, much less ones claiming to know his boss.

Slocum left and found that he needed a drink bad. The Tumbleweed Saloon looked as good as any. He pushed through the doors and cast an eye around the interior. It was too early in the afternoon for much of a crowd, but several men were playing faro at a table to his left, and a drunk sprawled across a green-topped table at the back of the saloon.

The bored barkeep perched on the edge of the bar. He frowned as Slocum came over. It meant he had to do even a minimal amount of work.

"What can I get for you?" asked the bartender.

"Whiskey, and none of that trade whiskey you foist off on the others," ordered Slocum. He glared at the muddy brown liquor in a bottle sitting on the back bar. He wondered what else they had put into it beside gunpowder, rusty nails, and cheap whiskey made in the back room.

"It'll cost you . . . a dollar," the man said, sizing Slocum up.

Slocum dropped a cartwheel on the bar and let it ring. The barkeep smiled for the first time and whisked the silver dollar from sight. He poured from a special bottle. Slocum reckoned the barkeep would pocket at least half the coin and probably pour water into the boss' special bottle to keep him from knowing anything had been removed.

"Can't say I've seen you around here," the barkeep said.

"I'm looking for some friends," Slocum said in a voice intended to convey that they weren't friends.

"You a bounty hunter?"

"Doesn't matter. I'm looking for a tall, scrawny fellow by the name of Ogelvie. He's likely to be with two others—"

"Ballard and Delling?"

"You know them?" This put Slocum on his guard. He had reckoned to pay at least ten dollars for the information. The barkeep was giving it to him for the price of a drink.

"Everybody in the whole damn town does, mister. If'n you're looking to take them back for some highfalutin reward, you're shit out of luck."

"Why's that?"

"We got an Arizona Ranger here name of Buck Johnson. He caught up with them hours after they robbed the bank."

"And?"

"And that's all there is. Ogelvie and Ballard were hanged a day or two after the robbery."

"And Delling?"

The barkeep snorted. "Johnson let that slimy son of a bitch go prancin' off scot-free."

"Now why would a law-abiding, upstanding Ranger do that?" Slocum asked. He knew the answer but wanted to hear it from the barkeep.

"Delling told him about the ringleader. That son of a bitch hightailed it down into Mexico with all the money from the robbery. In return for a good description and their meetin' place, Delling got off without even havin' to stand trial."

Slocum heaved a deep sigh. It hadn't worked out the way he'd thought it might. Ogelvie had been the one he'd have bet put the Ranger on his trail. But it had been the pudgy, frightened Delling. He'd squawked to save his own hide.

"If they got what's coming to them, I reckon there's no need for me to stay around here." Slocum finished his drink and had started for the door when the barkeep called out to him.

"If you got a warrant on Delling, you might be able to serve it. That lowlife is still here in Nogales."

"Do tell," Slocum said, feigning disinterest.

"Can't say for sure, but I reckon he's got the money from the bank robbery. Not a cent of it was recovered. Delling claimed Ogelvie made off with it when the posse was chasing them. Didn't know what happened to it, or so he said."

"Might be that way," Slocum said. He left the saloon, thinking hard. Delling had the money when they'd split up, not Ogelvie. That meant Delling not only sold the other two out, he had hidden the money.

Delling had sold out two partners and tried to do the same to a third. Slocum decided it was time to settle accounts.

He found a chair on the boardwalk and rocked back against the saloon wall, his hat pulled down so he could watch as people passed in the dusty street. He waited less than an hour before Delling came waddling along the rickety boardwalk. He passed less than a foot from Slocum and never noticed him.

Slocum let the portly man go into the saloon before getting up to follow him. He peered through a dirty windowpane and saw Delling bellying up to the bar. The man looked to be settling in for a long night of drinking and carousing.

Slocum touched the ebony-handled six-shooter holstered at his left side and went into the saloon.

A silence fell and all eyes turned toward him. Delling choked when he saw who had entered.

The fear on Delling's fat face gave Slocum no pleasure. The fear faded and Delling rushed forward, hand stuck out.

"John! What a fine day this is for me. I never expected to see you again!"

"Reckon not," Slocum said. "I just rode in from Mexico."

Relief flooded over Delling. He thought Slocum was ignorant of all that had happened in Nogales.

"Come on outside, John. Let's talk," Delling almost babbled.

Slocum spun and followed the man outside. The sun had set, and the desert night was turning chilly.

"I can't believe it's you," Delling started. He paled when he saw Slocum's dark expression.

"So the Ranger gave you a full pardon for turning in Ogelvie and Ballard," Slocum said coldly. "And you told him about us meeting in Hermosilla."

"John, I didn't have any choice. It was them or me. And I swear, it wasn't me who told Johnson about the meeting in Hermosilla. It had to be Ogelvie or Ballard."

"Might have been," Slocum allowed.

Relief flooded Delling's face. "It was. It had to be."

"Where's the money?"

"What?" Fear again crossed Delling's florid face. "I don't have it. Ogelvie had it. He caught up with me and took it and—"

"You lying sack of shit," Slocum said.

Delling panicked at this. He went for his six-shooter. He was no match for John Slocum's blinding speed. Slocum got to his cross-draw holster and pulled the Colt and fired before Delling's pistol even cleared leather.

Delling stared at him blankly, then slumped to the dusty street, dead. Slocum went over to him and pushed open his jacket. Stuffed inside were a few greenbacks. What had happened to the rest of the robbery loot Slocum didn't know. Delling might have hidden it. If so, the hiding place had died with him.

Slocum took the few bills and let them slip from his fingers. The hot, dry night wind caught the bills and scattered them along Nogales' main street. Slocum turned and walked off without a backward look. Justice had been served.

Now he had to get his silver and figure out where to spend it. As he climbed into the saddle and his paint turned toward the desert and the buried Yaqui silver, Slocum decided California might not be such a bad place. He'd heard San Luis was an inviting place. With any luck, he might be there in a month.